THE BIG BROTHER SERIES.

CAPTAIN SAM

OR

THE BOY SCOUTS OF 1814

BY

GEORGE CARY EGGLESTON

Author of "The Big Brother," etc., etc.

NEW YORK:
G. P. PUTNAM'S SONS,
182 FIFTH AVENUE.
1876.

To my Boy-Friend

MONTAGUE DOUGLAS,

IN RECOGNITION OF HIS MANLY CHARACTER, AND IN MEMORY OF THE FOOT-JOURNEYS WE MADE TOGETHER A YEAR AGO,

I DEDICATE THIS BOOK.

CAPTAIN SAM.

CHAPTER I.

A MUTINY.

"IF you open your mouth again, I'll drive my fist down your throat!"

The young man, or boy rather,—for he was not yet eighteen years old,—who made this very emphatic remark, was a stalwart, well-built youth, lithe of limb, elastic in movement, slender, straight, tall, with a rather thin face, upon which there was as yet no trace of coming beard, high cheek bones, and eyes that seemed almost to emit sparks of fire as their lids snapped rapidly together. He spoke in a low tone, without a sign of anger in his voice, but with a look of earnestness which must have convinced the person to whom he addressed his not very suave remark, that he really meant to do precisely what he threatened.

As he spoke he laid his left hand upon the other's shoulder, and placed his face as near to his companion's as was possible without bringing their noses into actual contact; but he neither clenched nor shook his fist. Persons who mention weapons which they really have made up their minds to use, do not display them in a threatening manner. That is the device of bullies who think to frighten their adversaries by the threatening exhibition as they do by their threatening words. Sam Hardwicke was not a bully, and he did not wish to frighten anybody. He merely wished to make the boy hold his tongue, and he meant to do that in any case, using whatever measure of violence he might find necessary to that end. He mentioned his fist merely because he meant to use that weapon if it should be necessary.

His companion saw his determination, and remained silent

" Now," resumed Sam, " I wish to say something to all of you, and I will say it to you as an officer should talk to soldiers on a subject of this sort. Fall into line! Right dress! steady, front!"

The boys were drawn up in line, and their commander stood at six paces from them.

"Attention!" he cried, "I wish you to know and remember that we are engaged in no child's play. We are soldiers. You have not yet been mustered into service, it is true, but you are soldiers, nevertheless, and you shall obey as such. Listen. When it became known in the neighborhood that I had determined to join General Jackson and serve as a soldier you boys proposed to go with me. I agreed, with a condition, and that condition was that we should organize ourselves into a company, elect a captain, and march to Camp Jackson under his command, not go there like a parcel of school-boys or a flock of sheep and be sent home again for our pains. You liked the notion, and we made a fair bargain. I was ready to serve under anybody you might choose for captain. I didn't ask you to elect me, but you did it. You voted for me, every one of you, and made me Captain. From that moment I have been responsible for everything.

"I lead you and provide necessary food. I plan everything and am responsible for everything. If you misbehave as you go through the country I shall be held to blame and I shall be to blame. But not a man of you shall misbehave. I am your commander, you made me that, and you can't undo it. Until we get to Camp Jackson I mean to command this company, and I'll find means of enforcing what I order. That is all. Right face! Break ranks!"

A shout went up, in reply.

"Good for Captain Sam!" cried the boys. "Three cheers for our captain!"

"Huzza! Huzza! Huzza!"

All the boys,—there were about a dozen of them—joined in this shout, except Jake Elliott, the mutineer, who had provoked the young captain's anger by insisting upon quitting the camp without permission, and had even threatened Sam when the young commander bade him remain where he was.

The revolt was effectually quelled. The mutineer had found a master in his former schoolmate, and forebore to provoke the threatened corporal punishment further.

The camp was in the edge of a strip of woods on the bank of the Alabama river, the time, afternoon, in the autumn of the year 1814. The boys had marched for three days through cane-brakes, and swamps, and had still a long march before them. Sam had called a halt earlier than usual that day for reasons of his own, which he did not explain to his fellows. Jake Elliott had objected, and his objection being peremptorily overruled by Sam, he had undertaken to go on alone to the point at which he wished to pass the remainder of the day, and the night. Sam had ordered him to remain within the lines of the camp. He had replied insolently with a threat that he would himself take charge of the camp, as the oldest person there, when Sam quelled the mutiny after the manner already set forth.

Now that he was effectually put down, he brooded sulkily, meditating revenge.

As night came on, the camp fire of pitch pine threw a ruddy glow over the trees, and the boys, weary as they were with marching, gathered around the blazing logs, and laughed and sang merrily Jake Elliott was silent and sullen through it all, and when at last Sam ordered all to their rest for the night, Jake crept off to a tree near the edge of the prescribed camp limits and threw himself down there. Presently a companion joined him, a boy not more than fourteen years of age, who was greatly awed by Sam's sternness, and who naturally sought to draw Jake into conversation on the subject.

"You're as big as Sam is," he said after a while, "and I wonder you let him talk so sharp to you. You're afraid o' him, aint you?"

"No, but you are."

"Yes I am. I'm afraid o' the lightning too, and he's got it in him, or I'm mistaken."

"Yes 'n' you fellows hurrahed for him, 'cause you was afraid to stand up for yourselves."

"To stand up for you, you mean, Jake. It wasn't our quarrel. We like Sam, if we are afraid o' him, an' between him an' you there wa'nt no call for us to take sides against him. Besides we're soldiers, you know, an' he's capt'n."

"A purty capt'n he is, aint he, an' you're a purty soldier, aint you. A soldier owning up that he's afraid," said Jake tauntingly.

"Well, you're afraid too, you know you are, else you wouldn't 'a' shut up that way like a turtle when he told you to."

"No, I aint afraid, neither, and you'll find it out 'fore you're done with it. I didn't choose to say anything then, but *I'll get even with Sam Hardwicke yet*, you see if I don't."

"Mas' Jake," said a lump of something which had been lying quietly a little way off all this time, but which now raised itself up and became a black boy by the name of Joe, who had insisted upon accompanying Sam in his campaigns; "Mas' Jake, I'se dun know'd Mas' Sam a good deal better 'n you know him, an' I'se dun seed a good many things try to git even wid him, 'fore now; Injuns, water, fire, sunshine, fever 'n ager, bullets an' starvation all dun try it right under my eyes, an' bless my soul none on 'em ever managed it yit."

"You shut up, you black rascal," was the only reply vouchsafed the colored boy.

"Me?" he asked, "oh, I'll shut up, of course, but I jist thought I'd tell you 'cause you might make a sort o' 'zastrous mistake you know. Other folks dun dun it fore now, tryin' to git even wid Mas' Sam."

"Go to sleep, you rascal," replied Jake, "or I'll skin you alive."

Joe snored immediately and Jake's companion laughed as he crept away toward the fire. An hour later the camp was slumbering quietly in the starlight, Sam sleeping by himself under a clump of bushes on the side of the camp opposite that chosen by Jake Elliott for his resting-place.

CHAPTER II.

GETTING EVEN IN THE DARK.

AM HARDWICKE had thrown himself down under a clump of bushes, as I have said, a little apart from the rest of the boys. Before he went to sleep, however, his brother Tom, a lad about twelve years of age, but rather large for his years, came and lay down by his side, the two falling at once into conversation.

"What made you fire up so quick with Jake Elliott, Sam?" asked the younger boy.

"Because he is a bully who would give trouble if he dared. I didn't want to have a fight with him and so I thought it best to take the first opportunity of teaching him the first duty of a soldier,—obedience."

"But you might have reasoned with him, as you generally do with people."

"No I couldn't," replied Sam.

"Why not?" Tom asked.

"Because he isn't reasonable. He's the sort of person who needs a master to say 'do' and 'don't.' Reasoning is thrown away on some people."

"But you had good reasons, didn't you, for stopping here instead of going on further?" asked Tom.

"Certainly. There's the Mackey house five miles ahead, and if we'd gone on we must have stopped near it to night?"

"Well, what of that?"

"Jake Elliott would have pilfered someth ng there."

"How do you know?" asked Tom in some surprise at his brother's positiveness.

"Because," Sam replied, "he tried to steal some eggs last night at Bungay's. I stopped him, and that's why I choose to camp every night out of harm's way, and keep all of you within strict limits. I don't mean to have people say we're a set of thieves. Besides, Jake Elliott has meant to give trouble from the first, and I have only waited for a chance to put him down. He isn't satisfied yet, but he's afraid to do anything but sneak. He'll try some trick to get even with me pretty soon."

"Oh, Sam, you must look out then," cried Tom in alarm for his brother. "Why don't you send him back home?"

"For two or three reasons. In the first place General Jackson needs all the volunteers he can get."

"Well, what else?"

"That's enough, but there's another good reason. If I let him go away it would be saying that I can't manage him, and that would be a sorry confession for a soldier to make. I can manage him, and I will, too."

"But Sam, he'll do you some harm or other."

"Of course he will if he can, but that is a risk I have to take."

"Well, I'm going to sleep here by you, any how," said Tom.

"No you mustn't," replied the elder boy. "You must go over by the fire where the other boys are, and sleep there."

"Why, Sam?"

"Well, in the first place, if I'm not a match in wits for Jake Elliott, I've no business to continue captain, and I've no right to shirk any trial of skill that he may choose to make. Besides you're my brother, and it will make the other boys think I'm partial if you stay here with me. Go back there and sleep by the fire. I'll take care of myself"

"But Sam—" began Tom.

"*You've* seen me take care of myself in tighter places than any that he can put me in, haven't you?" asked Sam. "There's the root fortress within ten feet of us. You haven't forgotten it have you?"

"No," said Tom, rising to go, "and I don't think I shall forget it soon; but I don't like to let my 'Big Brother' sleep here alone with Jake Elliott around."

"Never mind me, I tell you, but go to the boys and go to sleep. I'll take care of myself."

With that the two boys separated, Tom walking away to the fire, and Sam rolling himself up in his blanket for a quiet sleep. He had already removed his boots, coat and hat, and thrown them together in a pile, as he had done every night since the march began, partly because he knew that it is always better to sleep with the limbs as free as possible from pressure of any kind, and partly because he suffered a little from an old wound in the foot, received about a year before in the Indian assault upon Fort Sinquefield, and found it more comfortable, after walking all day, to remove his boots.

The camp grew quiet only by degrees. Boys have so many things to talk about that when they are together they are pretty certain to talk a good while before going to sleep, and especially so when they are lying in the open air, under the starlight, near a pile of blazing logs. They all stretched themselves out on the ground, weary with their day's march, and determined to go at once to sleep, but somehow each one found something that he wanted to say and so it was more than an hour before the camp was quite still. Then every one slept except Jake Elliott. He lay quietly by a tree, and seemed to be sleeping soundly enough, but in fact he was not even dozing. He was laying plans. He had a grudge against Sam Hardwicke, as we know, and was very busily thinking what he could do by way of revenge. He meant to do it at night, whatever it might be, because he was afraid to attempt any thing openly, which would bring on a conflict with Sam, of whom he was very heartily afraid. He was ready to do any thing that would annoy Sam, however mean it might be, for he was a coward seeking revenge, and cowardice is so mean a thing itself, that it always keeps the meanest kind of company in the breasts of boys or men who harbor it. Boys are apt to make mistakes about cowardice, however, and men too for that matter, confounding it with timidity and nervousness, and imagining that the ability to face unknown danger boldly is courage. There could be no greater mistake than this, and it is worth while to correct it. The bravest man I ever knew was so timid that he shrunk from a shower bath and jumped like a girl if any one clapped hands suddenly behind him. Cowardice is a matter of character. Brave men are they who face danger coolly when it is their duty to do so, not because they do not fear danger but because they will not run away from a duty. Cowards often go into danger boastfully and without seeming to care a fig for it, merely because they are conscious of their own fault and afraid that somebody will find it out. Cowards are men or women or boys, who lack character, and a genuine coward is very sure to show his lack of moral character in other ways than by shunning danger. They lie, because they fear to tell the truth, which is a thing that requires a good deal of moral courage sometimes. They are apt to be revengeful, too, because they resent other people's superiority to themselves, and are not strong enough in manliness to be generous. They seek revenge for petty wrongs, real or imaginary, in sly, sneaking, cowardly ways because—well because they are cowards. Jake Elliott was a boy of this sort. He was always a bully, and people who imagined that courage is best shown by fighting and blustering, thought Jake a very brave fellow. If they could have known him somewhat better, they would have discovered that all his fighting was done merely to conceal the fact that he was afraid to fight. He measured his adversaries pretty accurately, and in ordinary circumstances he would have fought Sam, when that young man talked to him as he did in the beginning of this story. There was that in Sam's bearing, however, which made Jake afraid to resist the imperious will that asserted itself more in the quiet tone than in the threatening words. He was Sam's full equal physically, but he had quailed before him, and he could scarcely determine why. It annoyed him sorely as he remembered the loud cheering of the boys. He chafed under the consciousness of defeat, and dreaded, the hints he was sure to receive whenever he should bully any of his companions, that he had a score still unsettled with Sam Hardwicke. He knew that he was a coward, and that the other boys had found it out, and he almost groaned as he lay there in the silence and darkness, meditating revenge.

A little after midnight he got up silently and crept along the river bank to the clump of bushes where Sam lay soundly sleeping. His first impulse was to jump upon the sleeper and fight him with an unfair advantage, but he was not yet free from the restraining influence of Sam's eye and voice so recently brought to bear upon him.

No, he dared not attack Sam even with so

great an advantage. He must injure him secretly as he had determined to do.

Creeping along upon all-fours, he felt about for Sam's boots, and finding them at last, was just about to move away with them when Sam turned over.

Jake sank down into the sand and listened, his heart beating and the sweat standing in great drops on his forehead. Sam did not move again, however, but seemed still to sleep. After waiting a long time Jake crept away noiselessly, as he had come.

Slipping down over the low sand bank he stood by the river's edge with the boots in his hand.

"Now," he muttered to himself, "I guess I'll be even with 'Captain Sam.' By the time he marches a day or two barefoot with that game foot o' his'n, I guess he'll begin to wish he hadn't been quite so sassy."

Filling the boots with sand he swung them back and forth, meaning to toss them as far out into the river as he could. Just as he was about quitting his hold of them, a terrifying thought seized him. The sand-filled boots would make a good deal of noise in striking the water, and Sam on the bank above would be sure to hear. Jake was ready enough to injure Sam, but he was not by any means ready to encounter that particularly cool and determined youth, while engaged in the act of doing him a surreptitious injury. He must go higher up the stream before putting his purpose into execution.

The bank at this point was crowned with a great pile of drift wood, the accumulation of many floods, which had been caught and held in its place by two great trees from the roots of which the water had gradually washed the sand away until the trees themselves stood up upon great root legs, fifteen feet long. The trees and the drift pile were the same in which Sam Hardwicke had hidden his little party a year before, when the fortunes of Indian war had thrown him, with Tom and his sister, and the black boy Joe, upon their own resources in the Indian haunted forest. The story is told in a former volume of this series.* Sam's resting place just now was within

* The Big Brother, published by G. P. Putnam's Sons. A friend suggests that many northern readers may doubt the existence

GETTING EVEN IN THE DARK.

a few feet of the great tree roots, but Sam was not sleeping there, as Jake Elliott supposed. He had been wide enough awake, ever since Jake first startled him out of sleep, and he had silently observed that worthy's manœuvres through the bushes. Jake crept along the edge of the drift pile to its further end, intending to toss the boots into the river as soon as he should be sufficiently far from Sam for safety. As he went, however, his awakened caution grew upon him. He reflected that Sam would suspect him when he should miss his boots the next morning, and might see fit to call him to account for their absence. He intended, in that case, stoutly to deny all knowledge of the affair, but he could not tell in advance precisely how persistent Sam's sus-

---

of such trees as those which I have described briefly here, and more fully in "The Big Brother." I think it right to explain, therefore, that I have seen many such trees with roots exposed in the manner described, in the west and south, and my favorite playing place as a boy was under precisely such a tree. Of course no tree could stand the sudden removal of ten or fifteen feet of earth from beneath it; but the trees described have gradually undergone this process, and the roots have struck constantly deeper, their exposed parts gradually changing from roots, in the proper sense, to something like a downward-branching tree trunk.

picion might be, and it seemed to him better to leave himself a "hole to crawl through," as he phrased it, if the necessity should come. He resolved, therefore, that instead of throwing the boots away, he would hide them so securely that no one else could possibly find them. "Then," thought he, "if the worst comes to the worst I can find 'em, and still stick to it that I didn't take 'em away." An opening in the pile of driftwood just at hand, was suggestive, and Jake crept into it passing under a great log that lay lengthwise just over the entrance. The passage way through the drift was a very narrow one but it did not come to an end at the end of the great log as Jake had expected, and he felt his way further. The passage turned and twisted about, but he went on, dark as it was. After a while he found himself in a sort of chamber under one of the great trees, and inside the line of its great twisted roots. He did not know where he was, however, but Sam or Tom or Joe could have told him all about the place.

Here his journey seemed to be effectually interrupted, and he thrust the boots, as he supposed, into a hole, driving them with some little force through a tangled net work of small roots. What he really did do, however, was to drive them through a net work of small roots, between two great ones, into the outer air, at the very spot from which he had taken them. When he quitted his hold of them, leaving them, as he supposed, buried in the centre of a great drift pile, they lay in fact by Sam's coat and hat, right where they had lain when Sam went to sleep.

Sam had silently observed him as he entered the drift pile, and running quickly to the entrance he seized a stick of timber and drew it toward him with all his force. Sam Hardwicke had an excellent habit of remembering not only things that were certainly useful to know, but things also which might be useful. When Jake entered the drift pile, Sam remembered that during his own stay there a year before, he had carefully examined the great log which formed the archway of the entrance, and that it was kept in its place only by this single stick of timber acting as a wedge. Pulling this out, therefore, he let the farther end of the great tree trunk fall, and completely blocked the passage way.

CHAPTER III.

REVENGE OF A DIFFERENT SORT.

NO matter where one begins to tell a story there is always something back of the beginning that must be told for the sake of making the matter clear. Whatever you tell, something else must have happened before it and something else before that and something else before that, so that there is really no end to the beginnings that might be made. The only way I can think of by which a whole story could be told would be to begin back at Adam and Eve and work on down to the present time; and even then the story would not be finished and nobody but a prophet ever could finish it.

The only way to tell a story then is to plunge into it somewhere as I did two chapters back, follow it until we get hold of it, and then go back and explain how it came about before going on with it. I must tell you just now who these boys were, where they were and how they came to be there. All this must be told sometime and whenever it is told somebody or something must wait somewhere, and I really think Jake Elliott may as well wait there in the drift-pile as not. He deserves nothing better.

During the summer of the year 1813, while the United States and great Britain were at war, a general Indian war came on which raged with especial violence in middle and southern Alabama. The Indians fought desperately, but General Jackson managed to conquer them thoroughly. He was empowered by the government to make a treaty with them and he insisted that they should make a treaty which they could not help keeping. He made them give up a large part of their land, and so arranged the boundaries as to make the Indians powerless for further harm.

The Indians hesitated a long time before they would sign the treaty, but it was Jackson's way to finish whatever he undertook, and not leave it to be done over again. As the people of the border used to say, he "left no gaps in the fences behind him," and so he insisted upon the treaty and the Indians at last signed it. Meantime, however, a great many of the Indians, and among them several of their most savage chiefs had escaped to Florida, which was then Spanish territory.

Jackson remained at his camp in southern Alabama through the summer of 1814 bringing the Indians to terms. During the summer it became evident that the British were preparing an expedition against Mobile and New Orleans, and Jackson was placed in command of the whole southwest, with instructions to defend that part of the country. This was all very well, and very wise, too, for there was no man in the country who was fitter than he for the kind of work he was thus called on to do; but there was one very serious obstacle in his way. He had his commission; he had full authority to conduct the campaign; he had everything in fact except an army, and it does not require a very shrewd person to guess that an army is a rather important part of a general's outfit for defending a large territory. He called for volunteers and accepted any kind that came. He even published a special address to the free negroes within the threatened district and asked them to become soldiers, a thing that nobody had ever thought of before.

The boys in the southwest were strong, hearty fellows, used to the woods, accustomed to hardship and not afraid of danger. Many of them had fought bravely during the Indian war, and when Jackson called for volunteers, a good many of these boys joined him, some of them being mere lads just turning into their teens.

Sam Hardwicke, was noted all through that country for several reasons. In the first place he was a boy of very fine appearance and unusual skill in all the things which help to make either a boy or a man popular in a new country. He was a capital shot with rifle or shot-gun ; he was a superb horseman, a tireless walker, and an expert in all the arts of the hunter.

He was strong and active of body, and better still he was a boy of better intellect and better education than was common in that country at that early day when there were few schools and poor ones. His father was a gentleman of wealth and education, who had removed to Alabama for the sake of his health a few years before, bringing a large library with him, and he had educated his children very carefully, acting as their teacher himself. Sam was ready for college, and but for Jackson's call for troops he would have been on his way to Virginia, to attend the old William and Mary University there, at the time our story begins. When it became known, however, that men were needed to defend the country against the British, Sam thought it his duty to help, and reluctantly resolved to postpone the beginning of his college course for another year.

All these things made Sam Hardwicke a special favorite, and persons a great deal older than he was, held him in very high regard, on account of his superior education, but more particularly on account of the real superiority which was the result of that education; and I want to say, right here, that the difference between a man or boy whose education has been good and one who has had very little instruction, is a good deal greater than many persons think. It is a mistake to suppose that the difference lies only in what one has learned and the other has not. What you learn in school is the smallest part of the good you get there. Half of it is usually worthless as information, and much of it is sure to be forgotten; but the work of learning it is not thrown away on that account. In learning it you train and discipline and cultivate your mind, making it grow both in strength and in capacity, and so the educated man has really a stronger and better intellect than he ever would have had without education. Many persons suppose,—and I have known even college professors who made the mistake,—that a boy's mind is like a meal-bag, which will hold just so much and needs filling. They fill it as they would fill the meal-bag, for the sake of the meal and without a thought of the bag. In fact a boy's mind is more like the boy himself. It will not do to try to make a man out of him by stuffing meat and bread down his throat. The meat and bread fill him very quickly, but he isn't fully-grown when he is full. To make a man of him we must give him food in proper quantities, and let it help him to grow, and the things you learn in school are chiefly valuable as food for the mind. Education makes the intellect grow as truly as food makes the body do so; and so I say that Sam Hardwicke's superiority in intellect to the boys and even to most of the men about him, consisted of something more than merely a larger stock of information. He was intellectually larger than they, and if any boy who reads this book supposes that a well-trained intellect is of no account in the practical affairs of life, it is time for him to begin correcting some very dangerous notions.

To get back to the story, I must stop moralizing and say that when Sam made up his mind to volunteer, a number of boys in the neighborhood determined to follow his example, and, as Sam has already explained, the little company was organized, under Sam's command as captain. Of course Sam had no real military authority, and he did not for a moment suppose that his little band of boys would be recognized as a company or he as a captain, on their arrival at Camp Jackson; but they had agreed to march under Sam's command, and he knew how to exercise authority, even when it was held by so loose a tenure as that of mere agreement among a lot of boys.

We now come back to the drift-pile. When Jake had carefully hidden Sam's boots, as he supposed, deep within the recesses of the great pile of logs and brush and roots, he began groping his way back toward the entrance. It was pitch dark of course, but by walking slowly and feeling his way carefully, he managed to follow the passage way. Just as he began to think that he must be pretty nearly out of the den, however, he came suddenly upon an obstruction. Feeling about carefully he found that the passage in which he stood had come to an abrupt termination. We know, of course what had happened, but Jake did not. He had come to the end of the log which Sam had thrown down to stop up the passage way, and there was really no way for him to go. He supposed, of course, that he had somehow wandered out of his way, leaving the main alley and following a side one to its end. He therefore retraced his steps, feeling, as he went, for an opening upon one side or the other. He found several, but none of them did him any good. Following each a little way he came to its end in the matted logs, and had to try again. Presently he began to get nervous and frightened. He imagined all sorts of things and so lost his presence of mind that he forgot the outer appearance and size of the drift pile, and frightened himself still further by imagining that it must extend for miles in every direction, and that he might be hopelessly lost within its dark mazes. When he became frightened, he hurried his footsteps, as nervous people always do, and the result was that he blacked one of his eyes very badly by running against a projecting piece of timber. He was weary as well as frightened, but he dared not give up his effort to get out. Hour after hour—and the hours seemed weeks to him,—he wandered back and forth, afraid to call for assistance, and afraid above everything else that morning would come and that he would be forced to remain there in the drift pile while the boys marched away, or to call aloud for assistance and be caught in his own meanness without the power to deny it. Finally morning broke, and he could hear the boys as they began preparing for breakfast. It was his morning, according to agreement, to cut wood for the fire and bring water, and so a search was made for him at once. He heard several of the boys calling at the top of their lungs.

"Jake Elliott! Jake! Ja-a-a-ke!!" He knew then that his time had come.

What had Sam been doing all this time? Sleeping, I believe, for the most part, but he had not gone to sleep without making up his mind precisely what course to pursue. When he threw the log down, he meant merely to shut Jake Elliott and his own boots up for safe keeping, and it was his purpose, when morning should come, to "have it out" with the boot thief, in one way or another, as circumstances, and Jake's temper after his night's adventure, might determine.

He walked back, therefore, to his place of rest, after he had blocked up the entrance of the drift-pile, and threw himself down again under the bushes. Ten or fifteen minutes later he heard a slight noise at the root of the great tree near him, and, looking, saw something which looked surprisingly like a pair of boots, trying to force themselves out between two of the exposed roots. Then he heard retreating footsteps within the space enclosed by the circle of roots, and began to suspect the precise state of affairs. Examining the boots he discovered that they were his own, and he quickly guessed the truth that Jake had pushed them out from the inside, under the impression that he was driving them into a hole in the centre of the tangled drift.

Sam was a brave boy, too brave to be vindictive, and so he quickly decided that as he had recovered his boots he would subject his enemy only to so much punishment as he thought was necessary to secure his good behavior afterward. He knew that the boys would torment Jake unmercifully if the true story of the night's exploits should become known to them, and while he knew that the culprit deserved the severest lesson, he was too magnanimous to subject him to so sore a trial. He went to sleep, therefore, resolved to release his enemy quietly in the morning, before the other boys should be astir. Unluckily he overslept himself, and so the first hint of the dawn he received was from the loud calling of the boys for Jake Elliott. Fortunately Jake had not yet nerved himself up to the point of answering and calling for assistance, and so Sam had still a chance to execute his plan.

"Never mind calling Jake," he cried, as he rose from his couch of bushes, "but run down to the spring and bring some water. I have Jake engaged elsewhere."

The boys suspected at once that Sam and Jake had arranged a private battle to be fought somewhere in the woods beyond camp lines, a battle with fists for the mastery, and they were strongly disposed to follow their captain as he started up the river.

"Stop," cried Sam. "I have business with Jake, which will not interest you. Besides, I think it best that you shall remain here. Go to the spring, as I tell you, and then go back to the fire, and get breakfast. Jake and I will be there in time to help you eat it. If one of you follows me a foot of the way, I—never mind; I tell you you must not follow me, and you shall not."

There were some symptoms of a turbulent, but good-natured revolt, but Sam's earnestness quieted it, and the boys reluctantly drew back.

Passing around to the further side of the drift-pile, more than a hundred yards away from the nearest point of the camp, Sam called in a low tone:—

"Jake! Jake!"

"What is it?" asked Jake presently, trembling in voice as he trembled in limb, for he was now thoroughly broken and frightened. He dreaded the meeting with Sam nearly as much as he dreaded the terrible fate which seemed to him the only alternative, namely, that of remaining in the drift-pile to starve.

"Come down this way," said Sam.

"Well," answered Jake when he had moved a little way toward Sam.

"Do you see a hole in the top, just above your head?" asked Sam.

"Yes, but I can't see the sky through it."

"Never mind, get a stick to boost you, and climb up into it."

Jake did as he was told to do, and upon climbing up found that there was a sort of passage way running laterally through the upper part of the timber, crooked and so narrow that he could scarcely force his way through it. Whither it led, he had no idea, but he obeyed Sam's injunction to follow it, though he did so with great difficulty, as in many places sticks were in the way, which it required his utmost strength to remove. The passage through which he was crawling so painfully, was one which Sam and his companions had made by dint of great labor, during their residence in the tree root cavern a year before. It led from the main alley way to their post of observation on top of the pile, their look-out, from which they had been accustomed to examine the country around, to see if there were Indians about, when they had occasion to expose themselves outside of their place of refuge. As the only way into this passage was through a "blind" hole in the roof of the main alley way, no one would ever have suspected its existence.

After awhile Jake's head emerged from the very top of the drift pile, and he saw Sam lying flat down, just before him. He instinctively shrank back.

"Come on," said Sam ; "but don't rise up or the boys will see us. Crawl out of the hole and then follow me on your hands and knees."

Jake obeyed, and the two presently jumped down to the ground on the side of the hummock furthest from camp.

Jake's first glance revealed Sam fully dressed, and standing firmly *in his boots.* There could be no mistake about it, and yet a moment before he would have made oath that those very boots were hidden hopelessly within the deepest recesses of the drift-pile. He could not restrain the exclamation which rose to his lips:—

" *Where* DID *you get them boots?* "

" Never mind where, or how. I have a word or two to say to you. You took my boots and were on the point of throwing them into the river. If you think such an act by way of revenge was manly and worthy of a soldier, I will not dispute the point. You must determine that for yourself."

" Let me tell you about it, Sam," began Jake in an apologetic voice.

" No, it isn't necessary," replied Sam. " I know all about it, and it will not help the matter to lie about it. Listen to me. You were about to throw the boots into the river; but you changed your mind. You know why, of course, while I can only guess; but it doesn't matter. You took them into the drift pile and put them into a hole there. The next thing you know of them I have them on my feet, and I assure you I haven't been inside the drift pile since you entered it. Solve that riddle in any way you choose. I blocked up the entrance, and this morning I have let you out. Not one of the boys knows anything about this affair, and not one of them shall know, unless you choose to tell them, which you wont, of course. Now come on to camp and get ready for breakfast."

With that Sam led the way. Presently Jake halted.

"Sam," he said.

"Well."

"My eye's all bunged up. What'll the boys say?"

"I don't know."

"What must I tell 'em?"

"Anything you choose. It is not my affair."

"They'll think you've whipped me?" exclaimed Jake in alarm.

"Well, I have, haven't I?"

"No, we hain't fit at all."

"Yes we have,—not with our fists, but with our characters, and I have whipped you fairly. Never mind that. You can say you did it by accident in the dark, which will be true."

"But Sam!" said Jake, again halting.

"Well, what is it now?"

"What made you let me out an' keep the secret from the boys?"

"Because I thought it would be mean, unmanly and wrong in me to take such a revenge."

"Is that the only reason?"

"Yes, that is the only reason."

"You didn't do it 'cause you was afraid?" he asked, incredulously.

"No, of course not. I'm not in the least afraid of you, Jake."

"Why not? I'm bigger'n you."

"Yes, but you're an awful coward, Jake, and nobody knows it better than I do, except you. You wouldn't dare to lay a finger on me. I could make you lie down before me and—Pshaw! you know you're a coward and that's enough about it."

"Why didn't you leave me for the boys to find, then, and tell the whole story?"

"Because I'm not a coward or a sneak. I've told you once, but of course you can't understand it; come along. I'm hungry."

CHAPTER IV.

A CERTIFICATE OF CHARACTER.

HREE or four days after the morning of Jake Elliott's release, Sam led his little company into Camp Jackson and reported their arrival.

As Sam had anticipated, General Jackson decided at once that the boys could become useful to him only by volunteering in some of the companies already organized, and Sam began to look about for a company in which he and Tom would be acceptable. The other boys were of course free to choose for themselves, and Sam declined to act for them in the matter. As for Joe the black boy, he knew how to make himself useful in any command, as a servant, and he was resolved to follow Sam's fortunes, wherever they might lead.

"You see Mas' Sam," he said, "you'n Mas' Tommy might git yer selves into some sort o' scrape or udder, an' then yer's sho' to need Joe to git you out. Didn't Joe git you out 'n dat ar fix dar in de drifpile more'n a yeah ago? Howsomever, 'taint becomin' to talk 'bout dat, 'cause your fathah he dun pay me fer dat dar job, he is. But you'll need Joe any how, an' wha you goes Joe goes, an' dey aint no gettin roun' dat ar fac, nohow yer kin fix it."

On the very morning of Sam's arrival, as he was beginning his search for a suitable command in which to enlist, he met Tandy Walker, the celebrated guide and scout, whose memory is still fondly cherished in the southwest for his courage, his skill and his tireless perseverance. Tandy was now limping along on a rude crutch, with one of his feet bandaged up.

Sam greeted him heartily and asked, of course, about his hurt, which Tandy explained as the result of "a wrestle he had had with an axe," meaning that he had cut his foot in chopping wood. He tarried but a moment with Sam, excusing himself for his hurried departure on the ground that he had been sent for by General Jackson. Having heard Sam's story and plans Tandy limped on, and was soon ushered into Jackson's inner apartment.

When the general saw him he exclaimed—

"What, you're not on the sick list are you, Walker?"

"Well no, not adzac'ly, giner'l, but I ain't adzac'ly a *walker* now, fur all that's my name."

"What's the matter?" asked Jackson.

"Nothin,' only I've dun split my foot open with a axe, giner'l."

"That is very unfortunate," replied Jackson, "very unfortunate, indeed."

"Yes, it aint adzac'ly what you might call *lucky*, giner'l."

"It certainly isn't!" said Jackson, a smile for a moment taking the place of the look of vexation which his face wore; "and it isn't lucky for me either, for I need you just now."

"I'm sorry, giner'l, if ther's any work to be done in my line, but it can't be helped, you know."

"Of course not. The fact is Tandy, I want something done that I can't easily find any body else to do. I'm satisfied now that the British are at Pensacola and are arming Indians there, and that the treacherous Spanish governor is harboring them on his *neutral* territory. I have proof of that now. Look at that rifle there. That's one of the guns they have given out to Indians, and a friendly Indian brought it to me this morning. But you know the Indians, Walker; I can't get anything definite out of them. I *must* find out all about this affair, and you're the only man I could trust with the task."

"I b'lieve that's jist about the way the land lays, giner'l," replied Tandy, "but I'll tell you what it is; if ther' aint a *man* here you kin tie to fur that sort o' work, ther's a purty well grown boy that'll do it up for you equal to me or anybody else, or my name aint Tandy Walker, and that's what the old woman at home calls me."

A little further conversation revealed the fact that the boy alluded to was none other than our friend Sam Hardwicke. General Jackson hesitated, expressing some doubts of Sam's qualifications for so delicate a task. He feared that so young a person might lack the coolness and discretion necessary, and said so. To all of this Tandy replied:—

"You'd trust the job to me, if I could walk, wouldn't you, giner'l?"

"Certainly; no other man would be half so good."

"Well then, giner'l, lem me tell you, that Sam Hardwicke is Tandy Walker, spun harder an' finer, made out'n better wool, doubled an' twisted, and *mighty keerfully waxed* into the bargain. He's a smart one, if there ever was one. He's edicated too, an' knows books like a school teacher. He's the sharpest feller in the woods I ever seed, an' he's got jist a little the keenest scent for the right thing to do in a tight place that you ever seed in man or boy. Better'n all, he never loses that cool head o' his'n no matter what happens."

"That is a hearty recommendation, certainly," said the general. "Suppose you send young Hardwicke to me; of course nothing must be said of all this."

"Certainly giner'l. Nobody ever gits any news out'n my talk." And with that Tandy made his awkward bow, his awkwarder salute, and limped away.

CHAPTER V.

SAM LAYS HIS PLANS.

HALF an hour later Sam Hardwicke entered General Jackson's private office, and was received with some little surprise upon the commander's part.

" Why, you're the young man who reported in command of some young recruits, are you not?" he asked.

Sam replied that he was.

" I didn't understand it so," replied Jackson, " when Walker recommended you for this service. However, it is all the better so, because *I* know your devotion, and Tandy has assured me of your competence. Sit down, our talk is likely to be a long one."

When Sam was comfortably seated, with his

hat "hung up on the floor," as Tandy Walker would have said, the general resumed.

"You understand of course," he said, "that whatever I say to you, must be kept a profound secret, now and hereafter, whether you go on the expedition I have in mind or not."

"You may depend upon my discretion, sir. I think I know how to be silent."

"Do you? Then you have learned a good lesson well. Take care that you never forget it. Let me tell you in the outset that the task I want you to undertake is a difficult and perhaps a dangerous one. It will require patience, pluck, intelligence and *tact.* Tandy Walker tells me that you have these qualities, and he ought to know, perhaps, but I shall find out for myself before we have done talking. I shall tell you what the circumstances are and what I wish to have done. Then you must decide whether or not you wish to undertake it; and if you do, you must take what time you wish for consideration, and then tell me what your plans are for its accomplishment. I shall then be able to judge whether or not you are likely to succeed. You understand me of course?"

"Perfectly, I think," replied Sam.

"Very well then. You know that a good many of the worst of these Creeks escaped to Florida, Peter McQueen among them. I could not pursue them beyond the border, because Florida is Spanish territory, and Spain is, or at least professes to be, friendly to the United States, and neutral in our war with the British. Now, however, I have good authority for believing that the Spanish Governor at Pensacola is treacherously aiding not only the Indians but the British also. A force of British, I hear, has landed there, and friendly Indians tell me that they are arming the runaway Creeks, meaning to use them against us. The Indians tell big stories, so big that I can place no reliance upon them, and what I want is accurate information about affairs at Pensacola. If there is a British force there, it means to make an attack on Mobile or New Orleans. I must know the exact facts, whatever they are, so that I may take proper precautions. I must know the size of the force, the number of their ships, and on what terms they have been received by the Spaniards. If they are made welcome at Pensacola, and permitted by the Spaniards to make that a convenient base of operations against us, the goverment may see fit to authorize me to break up the hornet's nest before the swarm gets too big to be handled safely. However, that is another matter. What I want is positive information of the exact facts, whatever they are. The difficulties in the way are great. We are at peace with Spain, and must do no hostile act upon her soil. I cannot even send an armed scouting party to get the information I need. If you go, you must go unarmed, and even then you may be arrested and dealt hardly with. It will require the utmost discretion as well as courage, to accomplish the task, and I have no wish that you should undertake it if you hesitate to do so."

"I do not hesitate, sir," replied Sam, "if, after hearing my plan, you think me competent for the business."

"Very well then," replied the general, "when will you be ready to lay your plan before me?"

"I am ready now, sir," said Sam, "so far at least as the general plan is concerned; little things will have to be dealt with as they arise."

"Certainly. What is your plan in outline?"

"To go to Florida on a trapping and fishing excursion. I am not a soldier yet, and may go, if I like, peacefully into the territory of a friendly nation. I can take some of my boys with me, and camp by the water side. I can easily go into Pensacola and find out what is going on there. I shouldn't wish to be a spy, general, but this is scarcely that, I think. The enemy has been received by a power professing to be friendly. That power has given us no notice of hostility, and until that is done I see no impropriety in going into his territory for information not about his affairs at all, unless he is proving treacherous, which would entitle us to do that, but about those of our enemy, whom he should regard as an invader, however he may regard him in fact."

"You've read some law, I see," said the general.

"No sir," replied Sam, blushing to think how he had been expounding to the general, a nice point which that officer must understand much better than he did. "No sir, I have read no law except a book or two on the laws of nations, which my father said every gentleman should be familiar with."

"A very wise and excellent father he must be," replied Jackson, "if I may judge of him by the training he has given his son."

"Thank you, sir, in his name," answered Sam, rising and making his best bow.

"To come back to the business in hand," resumed Jackson. "You'll need a boat and some camp equipments."

"A boat, yes, but as for camp equipments, I can make out without them very well. I've camped a good deal and I know how to manage."

"Very well, then, you'll be all the lighter. How many of your boys will you need?"

"Two or three,—partly to make a show of a camp, but more because it may be necessary to send some of them back with news. My brother Tom and my black boy, with one or two others will be enough."

"Very well. Now you must be off as soon as possible. I shall march to Mobile in a day or two, and organize for defence there. Send your news there. You had better march directly from this place, so that your arrival will excite no suspicion. I will provide you with a map of the country. Have you a compass?"

"Yes sir, I brought one with me from home."

"There are boats enough to be had among the fishermen, I suppose, but how to provide you with one is the most serious problem I have to solve in this matter. My army chest is empty, and my personal purse is equally so."

"I can manage all that, sir, if I may take an axe or two and an adze from the shop here."

"How?"

"By digging out a canoe. I've done it before, and know how to handle the tools."

"You certainly do not lack the sort of resources which a commander needs in such a country as this, where he must first create his army and then arm and feed it without money. You'll make a general yet, I fancy."

"At present I am not even a private," replied Sam, "though the boys call me Captain Sam."

"Do they? Then Captain Sam it shall be, and I wish you a successful campaign before Pensacola, Captain. Get your forces into marching order at once. Take all of your boys, unless some of them have already enlisted,—it won't do to take actual soldiers with you, as your's must be a citizen's camp,—and march as early as you can. I'll see that you are properly provided with the tools you need."

CHAPTER VI.

CAPTAIN SAM BEGINS HIS MARCH.

AT noon the next day Sam marched away from the camp at the head of his little company, reduced now to precisely six boys in all, counting the colored boy Joe, but not counting Captain Sam himself. Jake Elliott was one of the company, rather against Sam's wish, but he had begged for permission to go, and Sam thought his size and strength might be of use in some emergency. Tommy was of the party of course, and the other boys were Billy Bunker—called Billy Bowlegs by the boys, because he was not bow-legged at all but on the contrary badly knock-kneed,—Bob Sharp, a boy of about Tommy's size and age, and Sidney Russell, a boy of thirteen, who had “r n to legs,” his companions said, and was already nearly six feet high, and so slender that, notwithstanding his extreme height, he was the lightest boy in the company. The rest of the party had already enlisted and could not go.

The outfit was complete, after Sam's notions of completeness; that is to say, it included every thing which was absolutely necessary and not an ounce of anything that could be safely spared. For tools they had two axes, with rather short handles, a small hatchet, a pocket rule and an adze; to this list might be added their large pocket knives, which every man and boy on the frontier carries habitually. For camp utensils each boy had a tin cup and that was all, except a single light skillet, which they were to carry alternately, as they were to do with the tools. Each boy carried a blanket tightly rolled up, and each had, at the start, eight pounds of corn meal and four pounds of bacon, with a small sack of salt each, which could be carried in any pocket. This was all. They had no arms and no ammunition.

Their destination and the purpose of their journey were wholly unknown to anybody in the camp, except General Jackson and Tandy Walker. The boys themselves were as ignorant as anybody on this subject. Sam had enlisted them in the service, merely telling them that he was going on an expedition which might prove difficult, dangerous and full of hardship. He told them that he could not make them legal soldiers before leaving, but that implicit obedience was absolutely necessary, and that he wanted no boy to go with him who was not willing to trust his judgment absolutely and obey orders as a soldier does, without knowing why they are given or what they are meant to accomplish. To put this matter on a proper basis, he drew up an enlistment paper as follows:—

"We, whose names are signed below, volunteer to go with Samuel Hardwicke and under his command, on the expedition which he is about beginning. We have been duly warned of the dangers and hardships to be encountered; we freely undertake to endure the hardships without shrinking, and to face the dangers as soldiers should; and, understanding the necessity of discipline and obedience, we promise, each of us upon his honor, fully to recognize the authority of Samuel Hardwicke as our Captain, appointed by General Jackson; we promise upon honor, to obey his command, as implicity as if we were regularly enlisted soldiers, and he a properly commissioned officer.

(Signed.)

Thos. Hardwicke
Jacob Elliott
Sidney Russell
William Bunker
Robt Sharp Jr
G. Butler

When this paper was signed by all the boys, including black Joe, who insisted upon attaching his name to it in the printing letters which "little Miss Judie" had taught him, it was placed in General Jackson's hands for keeping, and Sam marched his party away, amid the wondering curiosity of the few troops who were in camp. They knew that this party went out under orders of some sort from head quarters, but they could not imagine whither it was going or why. Many of them had tried to get information from the boys themselves, but as the boys knew absolutely nothing about it, they could answer no questions, except with the rather unsatisfactory formula "I dunno."

CHAPTER VII.

SAM'S TRAVELLING FACTORY.

THE boys marched steadily until sunset, when Sam called a halt and selected a camping place for the night. He ordered a fire built and himself superintended the preparation of supper, limiting the amount of food cooked for each member of the party, a regulation which he enforced strictly throughout the march, lest any of the boys should imprudently eat their rations too fast, which, as their route lay through woods and swamps in a part of the country scarcely at all settled, would bring disaster upon the expedition of course. Sam had calculated the march to last about ten days, but he hoped to accomplish it within a briefer time. The supplies they had would last ten days, and Sam hoped to add to them by killing game from time to time, for although the party were unarmed, Sam knew ways of getting game without gunpowder, and meant to put some of them in practice.

Toward evening of the first day out, he had stopped in a canebrake and cut three well seasoned canes, selecting straight, tall ones, about an inch in diameter, and taking care that they tapered as little and as regularly as possible. Cutting them off at both ends and leaving them about fifteen feet in length, he next cut three or four small canes, very long and green ones, without flaw.

That night, as soon as supper was over he brought his canes to the fire and laid them down, preparatory to beginning work upon them.

"What are you a goin' to do with them canes, Sam?" asked Billy Bowlegs.

"What do you think, Billy?"

"Dog-gone ef I know," replied Billy.

"Suppose you quit saying 'dog-gone' Billy," said Sam. "It isn't a very good thing to say, and you've said it thirty-two times this afternoon."

"Have I? well, what's the odds if I have?"

"Well, it's a bad habit, and if you'll quit it, I'll give you one of those canes when I get them ready."

" What 'er you goin' to make 'em into ? "

" Guns," said Sam, working away as hard as he could with his jack-knife.

" Guns ! what sort o' guns ? Powder'd burst 'em in a minute, and besides we aint got no powder."

" No, but I'm going to make guns out of these canes, and I'm going to kill something with them too."

" What sort o' guns ? "

" Blow guns."

" What's a blow gun, Mas. Sam ? " asked Joe, becoming interested, as all the boys were now.

Sam was too busy to answer at the moment and so Tom, who had seen Sam's blow guns at home, answered for him.

" He's going to burn out the joints and then make arrows with iron points and some rabbit fur around the light ends. The fur fills up the hole in the cane, and when he blows in the end it sends the arrow off like a bullet. But Sam ! " he cried, suddenly thinking of something.

" What is it ? " asked the elder brother without looking up.

"What are you going to burn them out with?"

"With that little rod," answered Sam, tossing a bit of iron about six inches long towards his brother, "I brought it with me on purpose."

"Well, but it won't reach; you've got to reach all the joints you know, and the rod must be as long as the cane."

"Oh no, not by any means."

"Yes it must, of course it must," exclaimed all the boys in a breath. "It's just like burning out a pipe stem with a wire."

"No it is not," replied Sam, smiling, "but suppose it is. I can burn out a pipe stem with a wire half as long as the stem."

"How?" asked two or three boys at once.

"By burning first from one end and then from the other."

"Yes, that's so," answered Sid Russell slowly, drawling his words out as if he had to drag them up through his long legs, "but that don't tell how you're goin' to bore out a big cane, fifteen feet long with a little iron rod not more 'n six or eight inches long."

"Well, if you will be patient a moment, I'll show

you," answered Sam, picking up the bit of iron. Trimming off the end of one of his small green canes, Sam measured it by the iron rod and trimmed again. He continued this process until he had the end of the cane a trifle larger than the iron was. Then taking an iron tube or band out of his pocket, he drove the iron rod firmly into it for the distance of about half an inch, leaving the other end of the tube open. Into this he forced the end of the small green cane and having made it firm he had a rod about ten feet long.

"There," he said, "I have a rod long enough to reach a good deal more than half way through either one of my big canes. It isn't iron except at the end, and it doesn't need to be," and with that he thrust the end of the bit of iron into the fire to heat.

"Now, Tom," he said, "you must burn the canes out while I do something else."

I wonder if there is any boy who needs a fuller explanation than the one which Sam has already given, of what was going forward. There may be boys enough, for aught I know, who never went fishing in their lives, and so do not know what canes, or reeds, or cane-poles, as they are variously called, are like. I must explain, therefore, that the canes which Sam proposed to burn out, were precisely such as those that are commonly used as fishing rods. These canes grow all over the South, in the swamps. They are, in fact, a kind of gigantic grass, although the people who are most familiar with them do not dream of the fact. The botanists call them a grass, at any rate, and the botanists know. Each cane is a long, straight rod, tapering very gently, with "joints," as they are called, about eight or ten inches apart. These joints are simply places where the cane, outside, is a little larger than it is between joints, while inside each joint consists of a hard woody partition, across the hollow tube, which is otherwise continuous. Sam's plan was simply to burn these partitions away with a hot iron, which would convert the cane into a long, slender, wooden tube, very hard, very light, and straight as an arrow.

Tom went to work at once to burn out the joints, a work which occupied a good deal of time, as the iron had to be re-heated a great many times. He worked very steadily, however with the assistance of two or three of the boys, and managed during that first evening to get two of the blow guns burned out.

Meantime Sam made an arrow, very small and only about ten inches long, out of some dry cedar.

"Now," he said, "I want those of you who are not busy burning out the canes, to go to work making arrows just like that, while I do something else."

The boys went to work with a will, while Sam, going into the nearest thicket, cut a green stick about three quarters of an inch in diameter. Returning to the fire, he split one end of this stick for a little way, converting it into a sort of rude pincer. He then unrolled his blanket, and revealed to the astonished gaze of his companions several pounds of horse shoe nails.

"What on earth are you goin' to do with them horse shoe nails?" asked Billy Bowlegs, looking up from the cedar arrow on which he was working.

"I'm going to make arrow heads out of them," answered Sam, thrusting several of them into the bed of coals.

With the side of an axe for an anvil, and the hatchet for a hammer, Sam was soon very busy forging his wrought nails into sharp arrow points, holding the hot iron in his wooden pincers. Among the things that Sam had thought it worth while to learn something about, was blacksmithing, and he was really expert in the simpler arts of the smith. He could shoe a horse, "point" a plow, or weld iron or steel, very well indeed.

He had learned this as he had learned a good many other things, merely because he thought that every young man should know how to do tolerably well whatever he might sometime need to do, and in a new country where shops are scarce and workmen are not always to be found, there is no mechanical art which it is not sometimes very convenient to know something about.

Sam wrought now so expertly that within less than an hour he had made six arrow points. These he fitted to six of the arrows, and then he suspended work for the evening, and marked progress on his map; that is to say, he pricked on his map with a pin the course followed during the afternoon, estimating the distance travelled as accurately as he could.

CHAPTER VIII.

A MOTION WHICH WAS NOT IN ORDER.

HE next day the march was resumed, and continued with some haltings for rest until about three o'clock, when Sam chose a camp for the night, saying that they had already made a better march than he had planned for that day, and that there was no occasion to break themselves down by going further.

The work was at once resumed upon guns and arrows, Sam beginning by finishing the arrows already made. He cut strips from a hare's skin which Tommy had brought with him at Sam's request, making each strip about four or five inches long, and just wide enough to meet around the end of an arrow. Binding these strips firmly, the arrows were complete. Each was a slender, light stick of cedar, shod at one end with a slender iron point, and bound around at the other, for a distance of several inches, with the fur of the hare. Pushing one of these into the mouth end of his blow gun, Sam showed his companions that the fur completely filled the tube, so that when he should blow in the end the arrow would be driven through and out with considerable force.

Pointing the gun toward a tree a little way off, Sam blew, and in a moment the arrow was seen sticking in the tree, its head being almost wholly buried in the solid wood.

The boys all wanted to try the new guns, of course, and Sam permitted them to do so, greatly to their delight, as long as the daylight lasted. Then the manufacture of new arrows began, the boys working earnestly now, because they were interested.

After awhile Sam took out his map and began pricking the course upon it.

"I say, Sam," said Bob Sharp, "how do you do that?"

"How do I do what? Prick the map?'

"No, I mean how do you know where we are and which way we go?"

"That's just what I want to know," said Sid Russell.

"And me, too," chimed in Billy Bunker and Jake Elliott.

"Well, come here, all of you," replied Sam, "and I'll show you. We started there, at camp Jackson,—you see, don't you, where the Coosa and the Tallapoosa rivers come together and we are going down there," pointing to a spot on the map, "to the sea, or rather to the Bay near Pensacola."

"Are we! Good! I never saw the sea," said Sid Russell, speaking faster than any of the boys had ever heard him speak before.

"Yes, that is the place we're going to, and presently I'll tell you what we're going for; but one thing at a time. You see the course is a little west of south, nearly but not quite southwest. The distance, in an air line is about a hundred and twenty-five miles: that is to say Pensacola is about a hundred and ten miles further south than camp Jackson, and about fifty miles further west."

"That would be a hundred and sixty miles then," said Billy Bowlegs.

"Yes," replied Sam, "it would if we went due

south and then due west, taking the base and perpendicular of a right angled triangle, instead of its hypothenuse."

"Whew, what's all them words I wonder," exclaimed Billy.

"Well, I'll try to show you what I mean,' said Sam, taking a stick and drawing in the sand a figure like this:

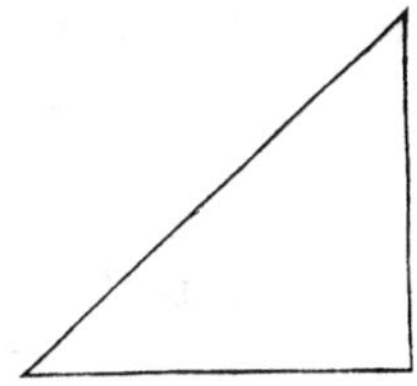

"There," said Sam, "that's a right angled triangle, but you may call it a thingimajig if you like; it doesn't matter about the name. Suppose we start at the top to go to the left hand lower corner; don't you see that it would be further to go straight down to the right hand lower corner and then across to the left hand lower corner, than to go straight from the top to the left hand lower corner."

"Certainly," replied Billy, "it's just like going cat a cornered across a field."

"Well," said Sam, pointing with his finger, "if I were to draw a triangle here on the map beginning at camp Jackson and running due south to the line of Pensacola, and then due west to Pensacola itself, with a third line running 'cat a cornered' as you say, from camp Jackson straight to Pensacola, the line due south would be about a hundred and ten miles long and the one due west about fifty miles long, while the 'cat a cornered' line would be about a hundred and twenty five miles long."

"How do you find out that last,—the cat a cornered line's length?" asked Tom.

"I can't explain that to you," said Sam, "because you haven't studied geometry."

"Oh well, tell us anyhow, if we don't understand it," said Sid Russell, who sat with his mouth open.

"Sid wants to find out how to tell how far it is from his head to his heels, without having to make the trip when he's tired," said Bob Sharp, who was always poking fun at Sid's long legs.

"Well," said Sam smiling, "I know the length of that line because I know that the square described on the hypothenuse of a right angled triangle is equal to the sum of the squares described on the other two sides."

"Whew! it fairly takes the breath out of a fellow to hear you rattle that off," replied Sid.

"Come," resumed Sam, "we aren't getting on with what we undertook. Now look and listen. Here is the line we would follow if we could go straight from Camp Jackson to Pensacola. If we could follow it, I would only have to guess how many miles we march each day, and mark it down on the map. But we can't go straight, because of swamps and creeks and canebrakes, so I must keep looking at my compass to find out what direction we do go; then I mark on the map the route we have followed each day, and the distance, and each night's camp gives me a new starting point."

"Yes, but Sam," said Tom, suddenly thinking of something.

"Well, what is it, Tom?"

"Suppose you guess wrong as to the distance travelled each day?"

"Well, suppose I do; I can't miss it very far."

"No, but it gives you a wrong starting-point for the next day, and two or three mistakes would throw you clear out."

"Yes, but I make corrections constantly. You see, I have changed the place of last night's camp a little on the map."

"How do you make corrections?"

"By the creeks and rivers. Here, for instance, is a creek that we ought to cross about ten miles ahead. If we come to it short of that, or if it proves to be further off, I shall know that I have got to-night's camp placed wrong on the map. I shall then correct my estimate. When we come to the next creek I shall be able to make my guess still more certain, and by the time we get to Pensacola I shall have the whole march marked pretty nearly right on the map."

"I'd give a purty price for that there head o' your'n, Sam," said Sid Russell.

"It isn't for sale, Sid, and besides it will be a good deal cheaper to use the one you have, taking care to make it as good as anybody's. Now let me explain to all of you why we are going to Pensacola," and with that Sam entered into the plans which we know all about already, and which need not be repeated here. When he had finished the boys plied him with questions, which he answered as well as he could. Jake Elliott said nothing for a time, but after a while he ventured to ask :—

" Don't they hang fellows they ketch in that sort o' business ? "

" They hang spies," replied Sam, " but they can scarcely hold us to be spies, especially as we shall be in the territory of a friendly neutral nation, where there cannot properly be a British camp at all."

" Well, but mayn't they do it anyhow, just as they are a campin' there, anyhow ? "

" Of course they may, but I do not think it likely. In the first place we mustn't let them suspect us, and in the second, we must make use of what law there is if we should be arrested."

" Well, but if it all failed, what then ? " asked Jake.

" Oh, shut up Jake," cried Billy Bowlegs. " You're afeard, that's what's the matter with you."

" Well," replied Sam " that is simply a risk

that we have to run, like any other risk in war. I told you all in advance that the expedition was a hazardous one."

"Of course you did, an' what's more you didn't want Jake Elliott to come either," said Billy Bowlegs.

"Go into your hole, Jake, if you're scared," said Bob Sharp.

"Jake ain't scared, he's only bashful,' drawled Sid Russell.

"I ain't afraid no more'n the rest of you," said Jake, "but you're all fools enough to run your heads into a noose."

"What do you mean by that?" asked Sam, looking up quickly from the map over which he had been poring.

"I mean just this," replied Jake, "that this here business 'll end in gettin' us into trouble that we wont git out of soon, an' I move we draw out'n it right now, afore its too late."

Sam was on his feet in an instant.

"Do you know what you're saying sir?" he cried. "Do you understand who is master here? Do you know that no motions are in order? Let

"DO YOU KNOW WHAT YOU'RE SAYING, SIR?"

me tell you once for all that I will tolerate no further mutinous words from you. If I hear another word of the kind from you, or see a sign of misconduct on your part, I shall take measures for your punishment. Stop! I want no answer. I have warned you and that is enough."

Sam's sudden assertion of his authority, in terms so peremptory, took Jake completely by surprise. Sam was a good tempered fellow, and not at all disposed to "put on airs" as boys say, and hence he had been as easy and familiar with his companions as if they had been merely a lot of school boys out for a holiday; but when Jake Elliott suggested a revolt, Sam, the good natured companion, became Captain Sam, the stern commander, at once.

The other boys saw at once the necessity and propriety of the rebuke he had administered. They believed Jake Elliott to be a coward and a bully, and they were glad to see him properly and promptly checked in his effort to give trouble.

It was growing late and the boys presently threw themselves down on their beds of soft gray moss and were soon sound asleep.

CHAPTER IX.

JAKE ELLIOTT GETS EVEN WITH SAM.

AKE ELLIOTT was a coward all over, and clear through. He had always been a bully and pretended to the possession of unusual courage. He had tyrannized over small boys, threatened boys of his own size and sneered at boys whom he thought able to hold their own against him in a fight. He had had many fights in his time, but had always managed to get the best of his opponents, by the very simple process of choosing for the purpose, boys who were not as strong as he was. As a result of all this he had acquired a great reputation among his fellows, and most of the boys in his neighborhood were very careful not to provoke him; but he was a great coward through it all, and when he first came in collision with Sam

Hardwicke his cowardice showed itself too plainly to be mistaken. Now there is a curious thing about cowards of this sort. When they are once found out they lose the little appearance of courage that they have taken such pains to maintain, and become at once the most abject and shameless dastards imaginable. That was what happened to Jake Elliott. When Sam conquered him so effectually on the occasion of the boot stealing, he lost all the pride he had and all his meanness seemed to come to the surface. If he had had a spark of manliness in him, he would have recognized Sam's generosity in sparing him at that time, and would have behaved himself better afterward. As it was he simply cherished his malice and resolved to do Sam all the injury he could in secret.

When Sam organized his expedition at Camp Jackson, Jake had two motives in joining it. In the first place things around the camp looked too much like genuine preparation for a hard fight with the enemy, and Jake thought that if he should enlist he would be forced to fight, which was precisely what he did not mean to do if he could help it. By joining Sam's party, however, he would escape the necessity of enlisting, and he thought that the little band was going away from danger instead of going into it. He thought, too, that if any real danger should come, under Sam's leadership, he could run away from it, or sneak out in some way, and as he would not be a regularly enlisted soldier, no punishment could follow.

This was his first reason for joining. His second one was still more unworthy. He was bent upon doing Sam all the secret injury he could, and he thought that by going with him he would have opportunities to wreak his vengeance, which he would otherwise lose.

When he learned, as we have seen, whither Sam was leading his party, and on what errand, he was really frightened, and Sam's sharp rebuke made him still bitterer in his feelings toward his young commander. A coward with a grudge which he is afraid to avenge openly, is a very dangerous foe. He will do anything against his adversary which he thinks he can do safely, by sneaking, and when Jake Elliott threw himself down on his pile of moss he did not mean to go to sleep. He meant to revenge himself on Sam before morning, and at the same time to make it impossible for the expedition to go on. If he could force Sam to return to Camp Jackson, he said to himself, he would humiliate that young man beyond endurance, and at the same time get himself out of the danger into which Sam was leading him. Everybody would laugh at Sam, and call him a coward, and suspect him of failing in his expedition purposely, all of which would please Jake Elliott mightily.

How to accomplish all this was a problem which Jake thought he had solved by a sudden inspiration. He had formed his plan at the very moment of receiving Sam's rebuke, and he waited now only for a chance to execute it.

An hour passed; two hours, three. It was after midnight, and all the boys were sleeping soundly. Jake arose noiselessly and crept to the tree at whose roots Sam had laid his baggage. It was thirty feet or more from any of the boys, and Jake was not afraid of waking them. He fumbled about in Sam's baggage until he felt something hard and round and cold. He drew out a little circular brass box about two and a half inches in diameter, with a glass top to it. It was Sam's compass. He tried hard to raise the glass in some way, but failed. Finally, with much fear, lest he should awaken some of the boys, he struck the glass with the end of his heavy Jack knife and broke it. This admitted his fingers, and taking out the needle of the compass he broke it half in two. Then replacing the brass lid, leaving all the pieces of the ruined instrument inside, he slipped the compass back into its original place and crept back to his bed by the fire.

"Now," he thought, "I reckon Mr. Sam Hardwicke's long head will be puzzled, and I reckon I'll be even with him, when he gives up that he can't go on, and has to turn back to Camp Jackson. A pretty story he'll have to tell, and wont people want to know how his compass got broke? They'll think it very curious, and maybe they wont suspect that he broke it himself, for an excuse. Oh! wont they though!"

He fairly chuckled with delight, in anticipation of Sam's humiliation. He knew that the country south of them was wholly unsettled, a perfect wilderness of woods and canebrakes and swamps, which nobody could go through without some guide as to the points of the compass, and hence he was satisfied that the destruction of Sam's instrument was an effectual way of compelling the young captain to retreat while it was still possible to retrace the trail the party had made in coming. He was so delighted that he could not sleep and hours passed before he closed his eyes.

CHAPTER X.

A DISTURBANCE IN CAMP.

AKE ELLIOTT got very little sleep that night. Indeed it was nearly daylight when he fell asleep and it was one of Sam's marching rules to march early. He waked the boys every morning as soon as it was sufficiently light for them to begin preparing breakfast, and by sunrise they were ready to begin their day's march.

This morning it was cloudy and there were symptoms of a coming storm. Sam was up at the first breaking of day, and he hurriedly waked the boys.

"Come, boys," he said, "we must hurry or we shall be too late to cross a river that's ahead of us, before it begins to rise. Get breakfast over as quickly as possible, for we mustn't fail to make seventeen miles to-day, and if it rains heavily it'll be bad marching in this swamp. There's higher ground ahead of us for to-morrow, but we mustn't be caught in here by high water in the creeks."

The boys sprang up quickly and made all haste in the preparation of breakfast. Jake Elliott was dull and moody. The fact is he was sleepy and tired with the night's excitement, and in no very good condition to march. He dragged with his share of the work, but breakfast was soon over, and Sam was ready to start. Taking out his compass to get his bearings right he opened it, and saw the ruin that had been wrought.

He looked up in surprise and caught Jake Elliott's eye. In an instant he guessed the truth.

"Lay down your bundles, boys," he said, "we cannot start just yet."

"Why not, Captain Sam?" asked two or three boys in a breath.

"Because Jake Elliott has broken our compass." replied Sam, looking the offender fixedly in the eye.

"Shame on the wretched coward," exclaimed the boys. "Let's duck him in the creek."

"I'm not a coward, and whoever says I broke the compass—"

"Silence!" cried Sam peremptorily. "Don't finish that sentence, Jake. It isn't a wise thing to do. Besides there's no use putting it in that way. 'Whoever says,' is a vague sort of phrase. You know very well who said that you broke the compass. I said it; Sam Hardwicke said it, and you do not dare to say that I lie. Don't try to say it by calling me 'whoever says.' That isn't my name."

Sam was as cool and quiet as possible. There was no sign of agitation in his voice, and no anger in his tone. The boys, however, were furious. They were in earnest in this expedition, and they supposed, of course, that the destruction of the compass would force them to return to camp. Beside this, it angered them to think that Jake had done so mean a thing.

Billy Bowlegs, the smallest boy in the party, was especially furious. Walking up to Jake with his fists clenched, he said:

"Jake Elliott, you're a sneak and a coward, and you daren't answer for yourself. Just deny it please, do deny it, so's I can bat you in the mouth. I'm hungry to wallop you. Do say I lie, or say anything, open your head, or lift your hand, or wink your eye, or look at me, or do something. Just give me any sort of excuse and I'll give you what you deserve, now and here."

Billy screamed this out at the top of his voice, advancing on Jake every moment, as the latter drew back.

"What can I say to make you fight?" he continued. "I'll call you anything that's mean. Just say what it shall be and consider it said. Won't any thing make you fight? *There*, and *there* and *there*, now may be you'll resent that."

The words "there and there and there" were accompanied by three vigorous slaps which Billy laid with a will on Jake's cheeks, in despair of provoking him to resent anything less positive. It was all done in a moment, and in another instant Sam had brought Billy Bowlegs to his senses, by quietly leading him away and saying.

"Let him alone, Billy; there's no credit in fighting such a coward."

Enough had occurred, however, to show that Jake was thoroughly scared by the little fellow's violence, and he could not have been more thoroughly whipped than he was already.

When order had been restored, Sam said quietly:—

"The breaking of the compass is a serious mishap, and the want of it will give us trouble all the way; but luckily it is not fatal to our expedition, if you boys will help me work out the problem without the aid of the needle."

"Help you! You see if we wont!" cried the enthusiastic boys in chorus.

"Thank you," replied Sam, lifting his cap, "I thought I could depend upon you."

"But can you really find the way without the compass, Sam?" asked Tom.

"Certainly, else I shouldn't be fit to be in the woods."

"How can you do it?"

"I'll show you presently."

"What'll you do with Jake?" asked Sid Russell.

"I'll take him with us," replied Sam.

"Is that all?"

"That is enough, I think. He is the worst punished boy or man in America this minute, and he'll be punished every minute while he stays with us."

" Well but ain't nothin' more to be done to him? Can't I just duck him a little or something of that sort?"

" No, certainly not. We all know him now, as a coward and a miserable sneak. What's the good of demonstrating it further? It would be dirtying your own hands."

" That's kind o' so, captain, but I'd sort o' like to duck him a little anyhow. The creek's so handy down there."

" No," said Sam. " I want no further reference made to this matter. Jake Elliott will go on with us, and as I have said already, he's punished enough. Besides it may prove to be a lesson to him. He may do better hereafter, and if he does, if he shows a genuine disposition to atone for his misconduct by good behavior in the future, I want nobody to tell of what has occurred here, after we get back to our friends. I ask that now of you boys as a favor, and I shall think nobody my friend who will not join me in this effort to make a man out of our companion. I am ready to forgive him freely, and the quarrel has been mine from the first. You can certainly afford to hold your tongues at my request, if Jake tries to do better hereafter. I want your promise to that effect."

The boys required some urging before they would promise, but their admiration for Sam's magnanimity was too great for them to persist in refusing anything that he asked of them. They promised at last, not only not to refer to the matter during their campaign, but to keep it a secret afterward, provided Jake should be guilty of no further misconduct.

"Thank you, boys," said Sam, "and now, Jake," he continued, "you have a chance to redeem your reputation. You cannot undo what you have done, but you can act like a man hereafter, without having this business thrown up to you."

Sam held out his hand, but Jake pretended not to see it.

CHAPTER XI.

BACKWOODS GEOMETRY.

HE quarrel having ended in the way described in the last chapter, the boys were compelled to find something else to talk about, as they were under a pledge not to refer further to that matter. They were prepared, therefore, to take an interest in Sam's preparations for resuming the march without the assistance of a compass. Their curiosity was great to know how he meant to proceed, and it was made greater by what he did first.

The clouds were thick and heavy, as I have already said, so that there was no chance to look at the sun for guidance; but Sam Hardwicke was full of resources. He had a good habit of observing whatever he saw and remembering it, whether he saw any reason to suppose that it might be of use to him or not. Just now he remembered something which he had observed the evening before, and he proceeded at once to make use of it.

He cut a stick, sharpened it a little at one end, and drove it into the ground at a spot which he had selected for the purpose. Then he walked away twenty or thirty paces and drove another stake, sighting from one to the other, and taking pains to get them in line with a tree which stood at a little distance from the first stake.

"What are you doing, Captain Sam?" asked Bob Sharp, unable to restrain his curiosity.

"I am getting the points of the compass," replied Sam.

"Yes, but how are you a doin' it?" asked Sid Russell.

"Well," replied Sam, "I'll show you. Just before sunset yesterday I wanted to mark my map, and I sat down right here," pointing to a spot near the first stake, "because it was shady here. The trunk of that big tree threw its shadow here. Now the sun does not set exactly in the west in this latitude, but a little south of west at this time of year. The line of a tree's shadow, therefore, at sunset must be from the tree a trifle north of east. Now I have driven this stake" (pointing to the first one) "just a little to the right of the middle of the shadow, as I remember it, so that a line from the stake to the middle of the tree-trunk must be very nearly an east and west line. The other stake I drove merely to aid me in tracing this line. Now I will go on with my work, explaining as I go."

Taking his pocket-rule he measured off twenty feet east and west from his first stake, and drove a stake at each point.

"Now," he said, "I have an east and west line, forty feet long, with a stake at each end and a stake in the middle."

This is what he had:

"A north and south line will run straight across this, at right angles, and I can draw it pretty accurately with my eye, but to be exact I have measured this line as you see. Now I'll draw a line as nearly as I can straight across this one, and of precisely the same length."

He drew and staked the second line, and this is what he had:

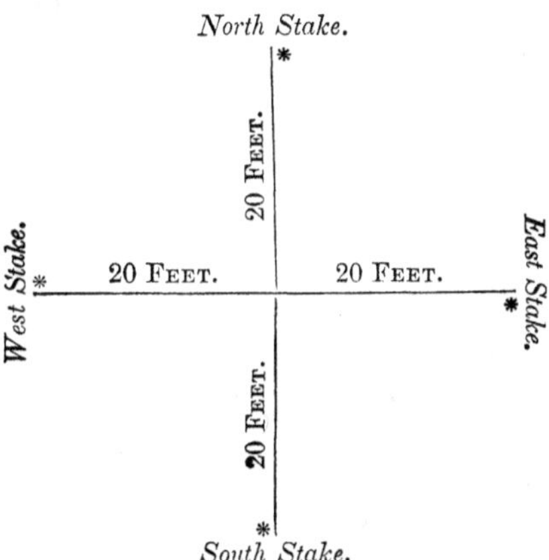

"Now," he said, "if I have drawn my last line exactly at right angles with my first one, it runs north and south; and to find out whether or not I have drawn it exactly, I must measure. If it is just right it will be precisely the same distance from the south stake to the east stake as from the south stake to the west stake; and from the east stake to the south one will be south-west, while from the west to the south will be south-east."

With that Sam measured, and found that he was just a trifle out. Readjusting his north and south stakes, he soon had his lines right.

"Now," he resumed, "I know the points of the compass, and I'll explain how you can help me. Our course lies exactly in a line from me through that big gum tree over there to the dead sycamore beyond.' If we go toward the gum, keeping it always in a line with the sycamore, we shall go perfectly straight, of course; and by choosing another tree away beyond the sycamore and in line with it, just before we get to the gum tree, we shall still go on in a perfectly straight line. We might keep that up for any distance, and travel in as straight a line as a compass can mark. Now if this country was an open one with no bogs to go around, and nothing to keep us from going straight ahead, I shouldn't need any assistance, but could go on in a straight line all day long. As it is, I must establish a long straight line, reaching as far ahead as possible, and then pick out two things in the line, one near me and one at the far end, which we can recognize again from any point. Then we'll go on by the best route we can till we come to the furthest object, and then I'll show you how to get the line again. What I want you to do is to notice the 'object trees' as we'll call them, so that we can be sure of them at any time. Notice them in starting, and as often afterward as you can see them. The appearance of trees varies with distance and point of view, and it is important that we shall be sure of our object trees and make no mistake about them."

"All right, Captain Sam," cried the boys, "pick out your object trees."

"Well," said Sam, "the big sycamore yonder will do for one, and that tall leaning pine away over there almost out of sight must do for the other. That is in our line, and what we've got to do is to get to it. It doesn't matter by how crooked a route, if we can remember the sycamore tree again and pick it out from there."

"We'll watch 'em captain, and we won't let 'em slip away from us," said Sid Russell.

"Thank you, boys," replied Sam; "I shall be so busy picking our way, that I can't watch them very well. Now then, we're ready, come on."

CHAPTER XII.

HOW TO HAVE A "LONG HEAD."

TWO hours steady walking, over logs and brush, through canebrakes, across a creek, and through a tangle of vines, brought the party to the leaning pine tree. From that point the old sycamore tree looked not at all as it did from the point of starting. The boys had taken pains to watch its changes of appearance, however, and were able to point it out with certainty to Sam.

"But what's the good of knowing it now?" asked Sid Russell, "we aint a goin' back that way agin'."

"No," said Sam, "but it is necessary to know it, nevertheless. How would you know which way to go without it, Sid?"

"Well, I'd pick out another tree ahead an' walk towards it."

"Well, but how would you know what tree to select?"

"Why I'd take one in a line with the pine."

"Well, every tree is in a line with the pine. It depends on where you stand to take sight."

"That's so; but how's the old sycamore to help us?"

"By giving us a point to take sight from. Let me show you. Our proper course of march is in the direction of a line drawn from the sycamore to this pine tree. What we want to do is to prolong that line, and find some tree further on that stands in it. If I stand on the line, between the sycamore and the pine and turn my face toward the pine, I'll be looking in exactly the right direction, and can pick out the right tree to march to, by sighting on the pine. The trouble is to get in the right place to take sight from. To do that I must find the line between the sycamore and the pine. Now you go over there beyond the pine, and take sight on it at the sycamore till you get the two trees in a line with you. Then I'll stand over here, between the two object trees, and move to the right or left as you tell me to do, till you find that I am exactly in the line between them. Then I can pick out the right tree ahead."

Sid did as he was told, the boys all looking on with great interest, and presently Sam had selected their next object tree. The boys were astonished greatly at what they thought Sam's marvellous knowledge, but to their wondering comments Sam replied :—

"I haven't done anything wonderful. A little knowledge of mathematics has helped me, perhaps, but there is'nt a thing in all this that isn't perfectly simple. Any one of you might have found out all this for himself, without books and without a teacher. It only requires you to think a little and to use your eyes. Besides you've all done the same thing many a time."

"I'll *bet* I never did," said Billy Bowlegs.

"Yes you have, Billy, but you did it without thinking about it."

"When?"

"Whenever you have shot a rifle at anything."

"How?"

"By taking aim. You look through one sight over the other and at the game, and you know then that you've got it in a line with your eye and the sights. I've only been turning the thing around, and nobody taught me how. You've only got to *use* your eyes and your head to make them worth ten times as much to you as they are now."

"Seems to me," said Sid Russell, "as if your head 'n eyes, or least ways your head is a mighty oncommon good one."

"You're right dah, Mas' Sid," said Black Joe; "you're right for sartain. I'se dun see Mas' Sam do some mighty cur'ous things, I is. He dun make a fire wid water once, sho's you're born. 'Sides dat, I'se dun heah de gentlemen say's how he's got a head more 'n a yard long, and I'm blest if I don't b'lieve it's so."

All this was said at a little distance from Sam and beyond his hearing, but he knew very well in what estimation his companions held him, and he was anxious to impress them, not with his own superiority, but with the fact that the difference was due chiefly to his habit of thinking and observing. He wanted them to improve by association with him, and to that end he took pains to show them the advantage which a habit of observ.

ing everything and thinking about it gives its possessor. For this reason he took pains to make no display of his knowledge of Latin or of anything else which they had no chance to learn. He wanted them to learn to use their eyes, their ears and their heads, knowing very well that the greater as well as the better part of education comes by observation and thinking, rather than from books.

Just now he was striding forward as rapidly as he could, as it was beginning to rain.

" Keep your eye on the hind sight boys, and don't lose it," he cried; " we must hurry or we shall be caught in a pocket to-night."

Hour after hour they marched, the rain pouring down steadily, and the ground becoming every moment softer. The walking wearied them terribly, but they pushed on in the hope that they might be able to cross the upper waters of the Nepalgah river before night. This would place them on the west bank of that stream, where Sam believed that he should find the marching tolerable. If they should fail in this, Sam feared that the water would rise during the night, and fill all the bottom lands. In that event he must continue marching down the east bank of the river; not going very far out of his way, it is true, but having to pass through what he was satisfied must be a much more difficult country than that on the other side.

Night came at last, and they were yet not within sight of the stream, notwithstanding their utmost exertions. Sam called a halt just before dark, and selected a camping place.

CHAPTER XIII.

WHAT DOES SAM MEAN?

HEN the halt was called, Sam said, very much to the astonishment of the boys:—

"We must build a house here, boys."

"A house!" exclaimed Tom, "What for, pray?"

"To live in, of course. What else are houses for?"

"Yes, of course, but aren't we going on?"

"Not at present, and it rains. We must dry our clothes to-night if we can, and keep as dry as we can while we stay here, which may be for a day or two. To do that we must have a house, but it need not be a very good one. Joe!"

"Yes, sah."

"Build a fire right here."

"Agin de big log dah, Mas Sam?" pointing

to the trunk of a great tree which had fallen in some earlier storm.

"No, build it right here. Sid, you and Bob Sharp go down into the canebrake there and get two or three dozen of the longest canes you can find."

"Green ones?" asked Bob.

"Green or dry, it doesn't matter in the least," answered Sam. "The rest of you boys go down into the swamp off there and cut a lot of the palmetes you find there,—this sort of thing," pointing to one of the plants which grew at his feet. "Get as many of them as you can, the more the better. The fire will be burning presently and will throw a light all around."

The boys were puzzled, but they hurried away to the work assigned them. Sam busied himself digging a trench on the side of the fallen tree opposite the fire. The great branches of the tree held it up many feet from the ground at the point selected, and it was Sam's purpose to make the trunk the front of his house, building behind it, and having the fire in front. The lower part of the trunk was high enough from the ground to let all the boys, except Sid Russell, pass under without stooping; Sid had to stoop a little.

The fire blazed presently, and by the time that Sam had his ditch done the boys began to come in with loads of cane and palmetes. The palmetes are plants out of which what we call "palm-leaf fans" are made. They grow in bunches right out of the ground in many southern swamps. Each leaf is simply a palm leaf fan that needs ironing out flat, except that the edge consists of long points which are cut off in making the fans.

Sam cut two forked sticks and drove them in the ground about ten feet from the fallen tree trunk, and about ten feet apart. When driven in they were about five feet high, while the top of the trunk was perhaps eight feet from the ground. Cutting a long, straight pole, Sam laid it in the forks of his two stakes, parallel with the tree trunk. Then taking the canes he laid them from this pole to the top of the tree trunk, for rafters, placing them as close to each other as possible. On top of them he laid the palmete leaves, taking care to lap them over each other like shingles. When the roof was well covered with them, he made the boys bring some armfuls of the long gray moss which abounds in southern forests, and lay it on top of the roof, to hold the palmete leaves in place, and to prevent them from blowing away. For sides to the house bushes answered very well, and in less than an hour after the company halted, they were safely housed in a shed open only on the side toward the fire, and the ground within was rapidly drying, while supper was in course of preparation.

" Sam," said Tom presently.

" Well," answered Sam.

" What did you dig that big ditch for? a little one would have carried off all the water that 'll drip from the roof."

"Yes, but I dug this one to carry off other water than that."

" What water?"

" That which was already in the ground that the house is built on. You see this soil is largely composed of sand, and water runs out of it very rapidly if it has any where to run to. I made the ditch for it to run into, and if you'll examine the ground here you'll find that my trench is doing its work very well indeed."

"That's a fac'," said Sid Russell, feeling of the sand.

"I say Sam," said Billy Bowlegs, squaring himself before Sam, with arms akimbo.

"Well, say it then," replied Sam, laughing, and assuming a similar attitude.

"If there is any little thing, about any sort o' thing, that you don't happen to know, I wish you'd just oblige me by telling me what it is."

"I haven't time, Billy," laughed Sam, "the list of things I don't know is too long to begin this late in the evening."

"Well, you've made me feel like an idiot every day since we started on this tramp, by knowing all about things, and doing little things that any fool ought to have thought of, and not one of us fools did."

"Come, supper is ready," replied Sam.

After supper the boys busied themselves drying their clothes by the roaring fire of pitch pine which blazed and crackled in front of the tent, making the air within like that of an oven. While they they were at it they fell to talking, of course, and it is equally a matter of course that they talked about the subject which was uppermost in their minds. They knew very well that until the house was built, and supper over, they could get nothing out of Sam. "He never will explain anything till every body is ready to listen," said Sid Russell, who had become one of Sam's heartiest admirers. Recognizing the truth of Sid's observation, the boys had tacitly consented to postpone all questions respecting Sam's plans and queer manœuvres until after supper, when there was time for him to talk and for them to listen. Now that the time had come, the long repressed curiosity broke forth in questions.

CHAPTER XIV.

SAM CLEARS UP THE MYSTERY.

OMMY was the spokesman.

"Now then, Sam," he said, holding out his trowsers toward the fire to dry them, "tell us all about it."

"I can't," replied Sam.

"Why not?"

"Because I don't know all about it myself."

"Well, what do you mean by building this shed?"

"Don't call it a shed, Tom," said Billy Bowlegs, "it's a mansion, and these are our broad acres all around here."

"Yes, and the alligators down in the swamp there are our cattle," said Sam.

"And here's our fowls," said Billy, slapping at the mosquitoes, "game ones they are too, ain't they?"

"Stop your nonsense," said Sid Russell, "I want to hear Sam's explanation. Tell us, Sam, what did you build the shanty for?"

"To live in while it rains, to be sure."

"Yes, but how long are we going to stay here?"

"I don't know."

"Well then, why are we to stop here at all?" asked Tom, "and what have you been thinking about all the afternoon? You didn't open your head after it began raining, until we got here; you were working out something, and this halt means that you've worked it out. What is it? That's what we want to know."

"You're partly right," said Sam, laughing, "but you're partly wrong. I have been thinking how to get out of this pocket we're caught in, and I've partly worked it out, but not entirely. That is to say, I must wait till morning before I can say precisely what I shall have to do. Let me show you where we are;" and with that Sam took out his map and spread it on the ground before him, while the boys clustered around.

"Here we are," pointing to a spot on the map,

"near the Nepalgah river, at the upper end of the peninsula it makes with the Patsaliga and the Connecuh rivers. You see the Patsaliga and the Nepalgah both run into the Connecuh, their mouths being not many miles apart. This peninsula that we're on is low, swampy, and full of creeks, a little lower down. This heavy rain will raise all the rivers and all the creeks, and make them spread out all over the low grounds on both sides. The land is higher on the other side of the Nepalgah river, and it was my plan to cross over to-day, but when this rain came on I began to think it not at all likely that we could get to the river before night, and then I began to lay plans for use in case of a failure."

"That's what you've been puzzling over all the afternoon, then?" said Bob Sharp.

"Yes. I've been wondering what we should do, and trying to hit upon some plan. You see the matter stands thus: we can't go on on this side, that is certain; the river will be out of its banks to-morrow morning, and we can't easily get across it; and if we were across it would still be difficult marching, as there are creeks and swamps enough to bother us over there."

"What are we to do, then?" asked Tommy, uneasily. "We *mustn't* go back. That'll never do."

"Never you mind, Tom," said Sid Russell, whose faith in Sam's fertility of resource was literally boundless, "never you mind. We ain't a goin' back if the Captain knows it. He's got it all fixed somehow in his head, you may bet your bottom dollar. Just wait till he explains."

"That's so," said Billy Bowlegs, "only it seems to me he's got a mighty hard sum this time, an' if he's got the right answer I'd like to see just what it is."

"He's got it, ain't you, Sam?" asked Sid, confidently.

"I believe I have," said Sam.

"What is it?" asked all the boys in a breath.

"Canoe," answered Sam.

"To cross the river with? that's the trick," said Bob Sharp.

"No," replied Sam, "that was what I first thought of; or rather, I first thought of building some sort of a raft to cross the river on, and then it occurred to me that we could go on faster on high water in a canoe than on foot; so my notion is to dig out a good big canoe and ride all the way in it."

"Can we do that?"

"Yes, the Nepalgah river runs into the Connecuh, and the Connecuh into the Escambia, and the Escambia runs into Escambia Bay, and Escambia Bay is an arm of Pensacola Bay. Here, look at it on the map; you see it's as straight a course as we could go even on land, or pretty nearly."

"Well, but you said you couldn't tell till morning about it."

"I can't. I am not absolutely sure where we are, but I think we are within a very short distance of the river. I shall look in the morning, and if we are, we'll dig the canoe here, or rather, we'll live here and dig the canoe down by the river, for it must be a big one to carry all of us, and we can't carry it any distance. If I find that we are not as near the river as I suppose, we must break up here and find a camping ground further on.

At all events we'll dig the canoe and ride in it. The rivers will be high, and it will be easy travelling with the current, while there won't be any danger of getting the fever from being on the water, as there would have been before the rain, when the water was low. Come, our clothes are dry now and we must go to sleep, as we've a hard day's work before us."

"How long will it take to dig out the canoe?" asked Bob Sharp.

"One day, I hope, but it may take as much as three. Luckily we've killed so much game to-day, that we needn't be afraid of running out of victuals. But we must lose no time."

"Oh, Sam—" began one of the boys after all had laid down for the night.

"I won't open my mouth again to-night, except to yawn," said Sam, and it was not long before the whole party were asleep.

CHAPTER XV.

A FOREST SHIP YARD.

DAY light had no sooner shown itself the next morning than Sam started away from the camp on a tour of observation. He was a fine looking fellow as he strode through the woods, straight as an arrow, broad shouldered, brawny, with legs that seemed all the more shapely for being clothed in closely fitting trowsers that were thrust into his long boot legs. Two of his companions watched him walk away in the early light.

"What a splendid fellow he is, outside and inside!" said Bob Sharp, half to himself and half to Jake Elliott, who stood by the fire. Jake said nothing and Bob was left to guess for himself what impression their stalwart young leader had made upon that moody youth. Meantime Sam had disappeared in the forest. He walked on for a little way when he came to a creek, a small one ordinarily, scarcely more than a crooked brook, but swollen now to considerable size.

"This may do," he said to himself. "At all events it leads to the river, and I may as well explore it as I go."

Accordingly he followed the stream. Mile after mile he walked, through bottom lands that were well nigh impassable now, never losing sight of the creek until he reached its point of junction with the river. It was still raining, but Sam persisted in the work of exploration until he knew the country thoroughly which lay between his camp and the river. Then he returned, not weary with his four hours' walking, but very decidedly hungry.

Luckily, Bob Sharp's enthusiastic admiration for his leader had taken a very prosaic and practical turn. It was Bob's turn to prepare breakfast, and a hare was to be cooked. The boys wanted it cut up and fried, but Bob remained firm.

"No, siree," he said, "Captain Sam's gone off to look out for us, without waiting for his breakfast, and when he comes back he's to have roast rabbit for breakfast, and his pick of the pieces at that. If any of you boys want fried victuals you may go and kill your own rabbits and fry them for yourselves, or you may cook your bacon. I killed this game myself, and nobody shall eat a mouthful of it till Captain Sam carves it."

The boys were hungry, but they agreed with Bob, when he thus peremptorily suggested the propriety of awaiting their young leader's return, and so when Sam got back, about ten o'clock, he found a hungry company and a beautifully roasted hare awaiting him, the latter hanging by a string to a branch of an over-hanging tree immediately in front of the fire.

After remonstrating with the boys in a good natured way, for delaying their breakfast so long, Sam carved, as Bob had put it; that is to say he held the hare by a hind leg, while another boy held it by a fore leg, and with their jack knives they quickly divided it into pieces, using the skillet for a platter.

The boys were not so hungry that they could

forget their curiosity as to the result of Sam's exploration.

"Where are we, Sam?"

"Did you find the river?"

"Is it close by?"

These and half a dozen similar questions were asked in rapid succession.

"One thing at a time," said Sam, "or, better still, listen and I'll tell you all about it without waiting to be questioned."

"All right, any way to get the news out of you," said Billy Bowlegs.

"Well then," said Sam, "to begin with, we're not very near the river. It's about five miles away, as nearly as I can judge."

Billy Bowlegs's countenance fell.

"Then we can't make the canoe here after all our work to build a house."

"I didn't say that, Billy. On the contrary, I think we must make it here, as there is no fit place for a camp nearer the river than this. Beside, the river will be out of its banks pretty soon if the rain continues, and will overflow all the low grounds."

"Then we've got to carry the canoe five miles! We can't do it, that's all," said Jake Elliott, who had not spoken before.

Sam looked at Jake rather sternly, and was about to make him a sharp answer, but changed his mind and said instead:—

"You and Billy are in too big a hurry to draw conclusions, Jake. Billy begins by assuming that because the river is five miles away we can't make the canoe here, and you jump to the conclusion that if we make it here we must carry it five miles. The fact is, you're both wrong. We can make it here, and we needn't carry it five miles, or one mile, or half a mile."

"How's that?" asked Tom.

"Now *you're* in a hurry, are you Tom? I was just about to explain and only stopped to swallow, but before I could do it you pushed a question in between my teeth."

"SILENCE!" roared Billy Bowlegs, "the court cannot be heard." Billy's father was sheriff of his county, and Billy had often heard him make more noise in commanding silence in the court room than the room full of people were making by requiring the caution.

Silence succeeding the laughter which Billy's unfilial mimicry had provoked, Sam resumed his explanation.

"There's a creek down there about a hundred yards, which runs into the river. It is a small affair, but is pretty well up now, and my plan is to make the canoe here and paddle her down the creek to the river while the water is high."

"Hurrah! now for work!" shouted the boys, who by this time had finished their breakfast.

"Where's your timber, Sam?" asked Tom, bringing the axes and adze out of the tent.

Sam had taken pains to select a proper tree for his purpose, a gigantic poplar more than three feet in diameter, which lay near the creek, where it had fallen several years before.

When the boys saw it, they looked at Sam in astonishment.

"Why, Sam, you don't mean to work that great big thing into a dug-out, do you?" asked Sid Russell.

"Why not, Sid?" asked Sam.

"Why, its bigger'n a dozen dug-outs."

"Yes, that is true, but we're not going to make

an ordinary canoe. We're going to cut out something as nearly like a yawl, or a ship's launch as possible. She is to be sixteen feet long, and three and a quarter feet wide amidships."

Sam had learned a good deal about boats during his boyhood in Baltimore.

"Whew! what do you want such a whopper for?"

"Well, in the first place such a boat will be of use to us down at Pensacola, where we couldn't use an ordinary canoe at all. You see I'm going to shape her like a sea boat, partly by cutting away, and partly by pinning a keel to her."

"What'll you pin it on with?" asked Tom.

"With pins, of course; wooden ones."

"What'll you bore the holes with?"

"With my bit of iron, heated red hot."

"That's so. So you can."

"But, Sam," said Sid.

"Well?"

"You said that was in the first place; what's the next?"

"In the next place, we'll need such a boat in running down the river."

"Why?"

"Because there'll be no fit camping places in the low grounds, even if the water isn't over the banks, and so we must stay in the boat night and day, which would be rather an uncomfortable thing to do in a little round bottomed dug-out, that would turn over if a fellow nodded. Beside that I'm anxious to make all the time I can and when we leave here I mean to push ahead night and day without stopping."

"How'll we manage without eatin' or sleepin'?" asked Jake Elliott, who seemed somehow to be interested chiefly in discovering what appeared to him to be insurmountable obstacles in the way of the execution of Sam's plans.

"I have no thought," answered Sam, "of trying to do without either eating or sleeping."

"Where'll we eat," asked Jake, "ef we don't stop nowhere?"

"In the boat, of course."

"Yes, but where'll we cook?"

"Here," answered Sam.

"Before we start?"

"Yes, certainly. We'll kill some game, cook

it at night and eat it cold on the way with cold bread. That will save our bacon to cook fish with down at Pensacola."

"Well, but how about sleeping?"

"That is one of my reasons for making so large a boat. We can sleep in her very comfortably, one staying awake to steer and paddle, all of us taking turns at it."

This plan was eagerly welcomed by the boys, who speedily fell to work upon the log under Sam's direction. The poplar was very easily worked, and the boys were all of them skilled in the use of the axes. Relieving each other at the work, they did not permit it to cease for a moment, and in half an hour the trunk of the tree was severed in two places, giving them a log of the desired length to work on.

Then began the work of hewing it into shape, and this admitted of four boys working at once, two with the axes, one with the adze and one with the hatchet. When night came the log had already assumed the shape of a rude boat, turned bottom up, and Sam was more than satisfied with the progress made. His comrades were enthusiastic, however, and insisted upon building a bonfire and working for an hour or two by its light, after supper. They could not work at shaping it by such a light, but they turned it over and hewed the side which was to be dug out, down to a level with its future gunwales. The next day they began work early, and when they quitted it at night their task was done. The boat was a rude affair but reasonably well shaped, broad, so that she drew very little water considering her weight, and with a keel which kept her perfectly steady in the water.

CHAPTER XVI.

CAPTAIN SAM PLAYS THE PART OF A SKIPPER.

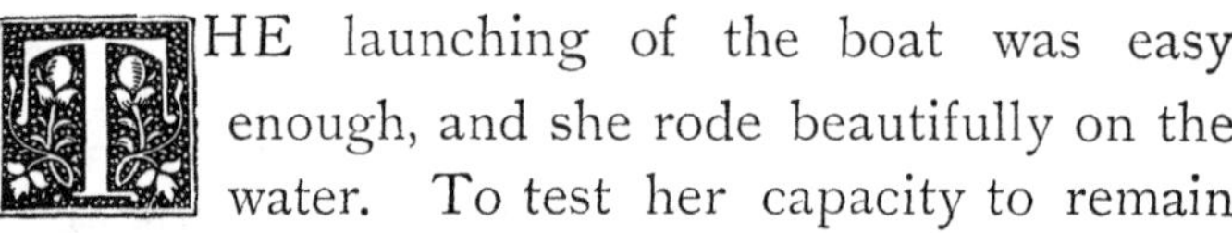

THE launching of the boat was easy enough, and she rode beautifully on the water. To test her capacity to remain right side up, Sam put the boys one by one on her gunwale, and found that their combined weight, thrown as far as possible to one side, was barely sufficient to make her take water.

The stores were stowed carefully in the bow and stern; rough seats were fitted in after the manner of a boat's thwarts, but not fastened. They were left moveable for the purpose of making it possible for several of the boys to lie down in the bottom of the boat at once. There was no rudder as yet, although it was Sam's purpose to fix one to the stern as soon as possible, and also to make a mast when they should get to Pensacola, where a sail could be procured. For the present two long poles and some rough paddles were their propelling power.

"When we get out into the river," said Sam, "she will float pretty rapidly on the high water, and we need only use the paddles to give her steerage, and to paddle her out of eddies."

"What are the poles for?" asked Tom.

"To push her in shoal water, for one thing," answered Sam, "and to fend off of banks and trees."

A large quantity of the long gray moss of the swamps was stored in the bottom for bedding purposes, and the boat was ready for her passengers. One by one they took their places, Sam in the bow, and the voyage down the creek began. This stream was very crooked, and many fallen trees interrupted its course, so that it was very difficult to navigate it with so long a boat. In addition to this, the river had risen much faster than the creek, and the back water had entirely destroyed the creek's current, so that the boat must be pushed and paddled every inch of the way.

Nearly the entire day was consumed in getting

to the river, five miles away from the starting place, and as the afternoon waned the boys grew tired, while Jake Elliott began to manifest his old disposition to criticise Sam's plans.

"May be we'll make five mile a day, an' may be we wont," he said. "We'll git to Pensacola in six or eight weeks, I s'pose, if we don't starve by the way, an' *if* this water runs that way."

"Very well," said Sam, "the longer we are on the route the better it will please you, Jake."

"Why?"

"Because you don't want to get there at all. But we'll be there sooner than you think?"

"How long do you reckon it will take us, Sam?" asked Billy.

"I don't know, because I don't know how long we'll be getting out of this creek."

"Well, I mean after we get into the river."

"About a day and a half," replied Sam, "possibly less."

"You don't mean it?"

"Don't I? What do I mean, then?"

"How far is it?"

"Less than a hundred miles."

"Well, we can't go a hundred miles in a day and a half."

"Can't we? I think we can. We'll run day and night, you know, and the current, at this stage of the water, can't be much less than five miles an hour. Four miles an hour will take us ninety-six miles in twenty-four hours."

"Hurrah for Captain Sam!" shouted Sid Russell, "Yonder's the river, an' she's a runnin' like a mill tail, too."

Sid was standing up, and his great length lifted his head high enough to permit him to see the rapidly running stream long before any one else did. The rest strained their eyes, or rather their necks trying to catch a glimpse of the stream, but the undergrowth of the swamp lay between them and the sight. Sid's announcement put new energy into them, however, and they plied their paddles vigorously for ten minutes, when, with a sudden swing around a last curve of the creek, Sam brought his boat fairly out into the river, and turned her head down stream. The river was full to its banks, and in places it had already overflowed. The current was so strong that the mouth of the creek, out of which they had come, was out of sight in a very few minutes. Work with the paddles was suspended, Sam only dipping his into the water occasionally for the purpose of keeping the boat straight in mid-channel. The river was full of drift-wood, some of it consisting of large logs and uprooted trees, and night was already falling. Jake Elliott now spoke again.

"We ain't a goin' to try to run in the dark in all this 'ere drift, are we?" he asked.

"I can't say that we are," replied Sam.

"Why, you're not going to stop for the night, are you, Sam?" asked Billy Bowlegs, who was enjoying the boat ride greatly.

"Certainly not," replied Sam.

"Why, you said you was, jist a minute ago," muttered Jake Elliott.

"Oh, no! I didn't," said Sam, whose patience had been sorely taxed already by Jake's persistent disposition to find fault.

"What did you say, then?" asked that worthy.

"Merely that we're not going to try to run in the dark to-night."

"Well, you're a goin' to stop then?"

"No, I am not."

"I see how dat is," said Joe, suddenly catching an idea.

"Well, explain it to Jake, then," said Sam laughing.

"W'y, Mas' Jake, don't you see de moon's gwine to shine bright as day, an' so dey ain't a gwine to be no dark to-night."

"That's it, Joe," replied Sam, "but if there was no moon I'd still go on. The drift isn't in the least dangerous."

"Why not, Sam?" asked Tom.

"Well, in the first place, it wouldn't be very easy to knock a hole in such a boat as this anyhow, and as we're only floating, we go exactly with the drift nearest us; we go faster than the drift in by the shore there, because we're in the strongest part of the current, but the drift nearest us is in the same current, and moves as fast as we do, or pretty nearly so. My paddling adds something to our speed, but not much. I only paddle enough to keep the boat straight in the channel. If we were to stop against the bank, and fasten the boat

SAM PLAYS THE PART OF SKIPPER.

there, the drift would bump us pretty badly, but it can do us no harm so long as we float along with it."

The moon, nearly at its full, was rising now, and very soon the river became a picture. Running rapidly, bank full, with tall trees bending over and throwing their shadows across it, with here and there a fragment of a moon glade on the water, while the dense undergrowth of the woods, lying in shadow, gave the stream a margin of inky blackness on each side,—it was a scene to stimulate the imaginations of the group of healthy boys who sat in the boat gliding silently but swiftly down the river.

Hour after hour they sped on, not a boy among them in the least disposed to avail himself of Sam's permission to lie down for a nap on the moss in the bottom of the boat. Every bend of the river gave them a new picture to look at, and finally Sam had to use authority to make the boys lie down.

"We must all sleep some," he said, "for to-morrow the sun will shine too strong for sleeping, and we've done a hard day's work. It will be now about seven or eight hours until sunrise, and there are just seven of us. It will take half an hour for the rest of you to get to sleep, and so I'll run the boat for an hour and a half. Then I'll wake Billy, and he can run it an hour. Then Joe must take the paddle,—his name is Butler, you see,—and so on in alphabetical order, each of you taking charge for an hour. If anything happens,—if you get into an eddy, or for any other reason find yourselves in doubt about anything, wake me at once. Now go to sleep."

Sam took the first watch, because he wished to see, before going to sleep, that everything was likely to go well. Then he waked Billy Bowlegs, and, surrendering the paddle to him, went to sleep.

There was no noise to disturb any one, and all the boys slept soundly, none of them more soundly than Sam, who had worked especially hard during the day, and had had a weight of responsibility upon him during the difficult voyage down the creek. He was quietly sleeping some hours later when suddenly the boat was sharply jarred, and turned very nearly on her side, while the water could be heard surging around her bow and stern.

Sam was on his feet in a moment, and the other boys sprang up quickly.

"Who's at the oar?" cried Sam, "and what's the matter?"

"We've got tangled in the drift, just as I told you we would," answered Jake Elliott from the bow, where he sat, paddle in hand, he being on watch at the time.

"Just as you meant that we should," answered Sam. "You've deliberately paddled us out of the current into a drift hammock, you sneaking scoundrel," continued Sam, now thoroughly angry, seizing Jake by the shoulders, and throwing him violently into the bottom of the boat. "I have a notion to give you a good thrashing right here, or to set you ashore and go on without you."

"Do it, Captain! Do it! He deserves it," cried the boys, but Sam had made up his mind not to give way to his temper, however provoking Jake's conduct might be, and as soon as he could master himself, he renewed his resolution, which had been broken only in the moment of sudden awakening.

The boat was not damaged in the least, but

her position was a difficult one from which to extricate her. She lay on the upper side of a pile of drift which had lodged against some trees, and a floating tree had swept down against her side, pinning her to the hammock, as such drift piles are called in the South. The work of freeing her required all of Sam's judgment, as well as all the boys' strength, but within half an hour, or a little more, the boat was again in the stream.

"Now," said Sam, speaking very calmly, "we've lost a good deal of sleep and must make it up. Jake Elliott, you will take the paddle again, and keep it till sunrise."

"Well, but what if he runs us into another snarl?" asked Sid Russell, uneasily.

"He won't make any more mistakes," replied Sam.

"How can you be sure of that?" queried Tom.

"Because I have whispered in his ear," said Sam.

What Sam had whispered in Jake's ear was this:—

"*If any further accidents happen to-night, I'll*

put you ashore in the swamp, and leave you there. I mean it."

He did mean it, and Jake was convinced of the fact. He knew very well, too, that if he should be left there in the swamp, with all the creeks out of their banks, the chances were a thousand to one against his success in getting back to civilization again. Sam's threat was a harsh one, but nothing less harsh would have answered his purpose, and he knew very well that Jake would not dare to incur the threatened penalty.

The boys slept again, and soundly. The night waned and day dawned, and still the current carried them forward. They breakfasted in the boat, first stripping to the waist and sluicing their heads, necks, arms and chests with water. Breakfast was scarcely over when the boat shot out of the Nepalgah into the Connecuh river, whereat the boys gave a cheer. About noon they entered the Escambia river, and their speed slackened. Here they had met the influence of the tide which checked the force of the current, and their progress grew steadily slower, until Sam directed the use of the paddles. They had long since left the drift wood behind, lodged along the banks, and they had now a broader and straighter stream than before, although it was still not very broad nor very straight. Two boys paddled at a time, one upon each side, while a third steered, and by relieving each other occasionally they maintained a very good rate of speed.

The moon was well up into the sky again when the river spread out into Escambia bay, and the boat was moored with a grape vine, in a little cove on one of the small islands in the upper end of the bay, about fifteen miles above Pensacola. The boys leaped upon land again gladly. Their voyage had been made successfully, and they were at last in the neighborhood of the danger they had set out to encounter, and the duty they had undertaken to do.

CHAPTER XVII.

THLUCCO.

HAT'S your plan now, Sam?" asked Tom, when the boat had been secured, and a fire built.

"First and foremost, where are we?" asked Sid Russell.

"Yes, an' how fur is it to somewhere else?" questioned Billy Bowlegs.

"An' is we gwine to somewher's or somewher's else?" demanded black Joe, with a grin.

"One question at a time," said Sam, "and they will go a good deal farther."

"Well, begin with Sid's question, then?" said Tommy. "His is the most sensible; where are we?"

"We're on an island," returned Sam, "and the island is somewhere here in the upper part of Escambia bay. You see how it lies on our map. The bay ends down there in Pensacola bay, and there is Pensacola, about fifteen miles away. We came here, you know, to find out what is going on in Pensacola and its neighborhood, and my plan is to run down past the town, to some point four or five miles below, in the neighborhood of Fort Barrancas. There I'll set up a fishing camp, but first I must get tackle, and, if possible, some duck cloth for a sail."

At this point the conversation was interrupted by the sudden appearance of a canoe's bow in their midst. Their fire was built near the water's edge, and the canoe which interrupted them had been paddled silently to the bank, so that its bow extended nearly into their fire.

"Ugh, how do," said a voice in the canoe, "how do, pale faces," and with that the solitary occupant of the canoe leaped ashore and seated himself in the circle around the fire.

Joe was frightened, but the other boys were reasonably self-possessed.

"Injun see fire; Injun come see. Injun friend."

"White man friend, too," said Sam, holding out his hand. "Injun eat?" offering the visitor some food.

"No. Injun eat heap while ago. Injun no hungry, but Injun friendly. Fire good. Fire warm Injun."

Sam continued the conversation, desiring to learn whether or not there was an Indian encampment in the neighborhood. He was not afraid of an Indian attack, for the Indians were not on the war path in Florida, but he was afraid of having his boat and tools stolen.

"Injun's friends over there?" asked Sam, pointing in the direction from which the canoe had come.

"No; Injun's friends not here. You know Injun; you see him before?"

"No," said Sam, "I don't remember you."

"Injun see you, all same. Injun General Jackson's friend. Injun see you when you come Gen eral Jackson's camp. Me go way then for General Jackson."

Here was a revelation. The young savage was, or professed to be, one of the friendly Indians whom General Jackson was using as scouts. It was certain that he had seen Sam on his entrance into General Jackson's camp, and he must have left immediately after Sam's arrival there.

"How did you get here so quick?" asked Sam.

"Me run 'cross country. Injun run heap."

"Where did you get your canoe?"

"Steal um," answered the Indian with the utmost complacency.

"Have you been here before?"

"Yes. Injun fish here heap. Injun go fishin' to-morrow."

"Where will you get lines and hooks."

"Me got um."

"Where did you get them?"

"Steal um," answered he again.

"We're going fishing, too," said Sam.

"You got hooks? You got lines? You got bait?"

"No," said Sam.

"Injun get um for you."

"How?"

"Steal um."

"No," said Sam, "you mustn't steal for us. I'll go to Pensacola and buy what I want. But you may go with us, if you will, and show us where to fish."

"Me go. Injun show you,—down there," pointing down the bay, "heap fish there."

The Indian, Sam was disposed to think, was a valuable acquisition, although he was not disposed to trust him with a knowledge of the real nature of his mission. Warning the boys, therefore, not to reveal the secret, he admitted the Indian, whose name was Thlucco, to his company, not as a member, but as a sort of guide.

The next morning the boat went down the bay to the town, where Sam stopped to purchase certain necessary supplies, chiefly fishing tackle and the materials for making a sail, and to take observations.

He found many British officers and soldiers lounging around the town, and had no difficulty in discovering that they were made heartily welcome by the Spanish authorities, notwithstanding the professed neutrality of Spain. It was clear enough that while the Spaniards were at peace with us, they were permitting our enemy to make their territory his base of supplies, and a convenient starting point of military and naval operations against us. All this was in violation of every law of neutrality, and it fully justified Jackson in invading Florida, and driving the British out of Pensacola, as he did, not very long afterward.

Sam "pottered around," as he expressed it, making his purchases as deliberately as possible, and neglecting no opportunity to learn what he could, with eyes and ears wide open.

In an open square he saw a sight which astonished him not a little. Captain Woodbine, a British officer in full uniform, was endeavoring to drill a band of Indians, whom he had dressed in red coats and trowsers. A more ridiculous performance was never seen anywhere, and only an officer like Captain Woodbine, who knew absolutely nothing of the habits and character of the American Indian, would ever have thought of attempting to make regularly drilled and uniformed soldiers out of men of that race. They were excellent fighters, in their own savage way, but no amount of drilling could turn them into soldiers of the civilized pattern.

It was a cruel, inhuman thing to think of setting these savages against the Americans at all, for their notion of war was simply to murder men, women and children indiscriminately, and to burn houses and take scalps ; but to try to make soldiers out of them was in a high degree ridiculous, and Sam could scarcely restrain his disposition to laugh aloud, as he saw them floundering about in trowsers for the first time in their lives and trying to make out what it all meant.

Thlucco, wrapped in his blanket, bare-headed and bare-footed, looked at the performance with an expression of profound contempt on his face.

"Red-coat-big-hat-white man big fool!" was the only comment he had to make upon Captain Woodbine and his drill.

Having bought what he wanted, and learned what he could, Sam returned to his boat, and paddled down the bay to a point not far from Fort Barrancas. Here he established his fishing camp, and began work upon his rudder, mast and sail. Before the evening was over he had his boat ready for sea, and was prepared to begin the work of fishing the next morning. He had news for General Jackson; and before going to sleep he wrote his first despatch.

CHAPTER XVIII.

"INJUN NO FOOL."

AM'S despatch, written by the light of a few pine knots and with as much care as if it had been an important state paper, —for whatever Sam Hardwicke did he tried to do well,—was in these words:—

To Major General Jackson,
Commanding Department of the South-West,
Mobile, Alabama.

General:

I arrived with my party to-day. In Pensacola, I found the British hospitably entertained, not only by the people, but by Governor Mauriquez himself. They are actually enlisting the savages in their service, arming them with rifles and knives and attempting to make regular soldiers out of them. I saw a British captain drilling about fifty Indians in the public square of the town at noon to-day.

I beg to report, also, that the British occupy the defensive works of the town, including Fort Barrancas, from the flagstaffs of which float both the British and the Spanish ensigns, as if the two were allies in this war.

I am unable to report as yet what the strength of the British force here is. I have observed men from seven different companies, in the streets, but have been unable to learn, without direct inquiry, which would excite suspicion, whether all these companies are present in full strength, or whether there are also others here.

The ships in the bay, so far as I can make them out, are the Hermes, Captain Percy, 22 guns; the Sophia, Captain Lockyer, 18 guns; the Carron, 20 guns; and the Childers, 18 guns.

I shall diligently seek to discover the plans and purposes of the expedition, and will not neglect to report to you promptly, whatever I may be able to find out. At present it is evident only that an expedition is fitting out here against some point on our coast.

I shall send this by a trusty messenger at daybreak.

All of which is respectfully submitted.

(Signed,)

SAMUEL HARDWICKE,
Commanding Scouting Party.

This document was duly dated from "Fishing Camp, Five miles below Pensacola," and when it was written, Sam quietly waked Bob Sharp.

"Bob," he said, "I have an important duty for you to do."

"I'm your man, Sam, for anything that turns up."

"Yes, I know that," replied Sam, "and that is why I picked you out for this business. The choice lay between you and Sid Russell, and I chose you, because I shall need a very rapid walker a little later to carry a still more important despatch, I fancy."

"It's a despatch, then," said Bob.

"Yes, a despatch to General Jackson. You'll find him at Mobile, and it isn't more than sixty or seventy miles across the country. I bought three compasses in Pensacola to-day, and you can take one of them with you. I can't give you my map, but I'll copy it for you on a sheet of paper. Go to bed now, and be ready to start at daylight. I'll cook up some food for you, so that you needn't stop on the way to do any cooking. You must make the distance in the shortest time you can!"

"After delivering the despatch, then what?" asked Bob.

"Well, if you want to, you can come back here."

"Of course I want to," said Bob.

"But you must rest first, and I'm not at all sure that you'll find us here. Perhaps you'd better wait in Mobile, at least till my next despatch comes. Then General Jackson will tell you what to do."

"If you'll just give me permission to start right back, I'll be here in a week. I kin make twenty-five miles a day, easy, an' that'll more 'n git me back here in that time."

"Very well, come back then."

At daylight Bob was off, and when the boys awoke they were full of curiosity to know the meaning of his absence. While Thlucco was around Sam would tell them nothing except that he had sent Bob away on an errand. When Thlucco went to the boat to arrange something about the fishing tackle, Sam briefly explained the matter, and cautioned the boys to talk of it no more.

An hour later they went fishing on a slack tide, and when it turned and began to run too full for the fish to bite they sailed their boat to the shore, with fish enough in it to satisfy the most eager of fishermen.

During the afternoon Sam sent Sid Russell, into the town, nominally to buy some trifling thing but really with secret instructions to find out what he could about the British forces, their movements, their purposes and their plans.

"Injun go town, too," said Thlucco, and without more ado "Injun" went.

When he returned, about ten o'clock that night, he brought with him a gun of superior workmanship, and a pouch full of ammunition.

"Where did you get that?" asked Sam in surprise.

"Pensacola," said the young savage.

"How?"

"Injun 'list. Big-hat-red-coat-white man give Injun gun, drill Injun."

"What in the world did you do that for?" asked Sam.

"Um. Injun got eyes. Sam got no guns. Sam need um. Injun git um. Injun 'list agin. Big-hat-red-coat-white man give Injun 'nother gun. Injun 'list six, seven times, git guns for boys."

"But we don't want any guns, Thlucco."

"Um. Injun no fool. Sam Jackson man. Injun know. Sam Jackson man. Boys Jackson men. Sam find out things, boys go tell Jackson. Bob go first. Um. Injun no fool. Injun Jackson man. Injun git guns, heap."

" But what can we do with them when you get them, Thlucco?"

" Um. Injun no fool. May be red coat men spy Sam. Sam caught. Sam want guns. Um. Injun no fool."

Sam saw that it was useless to prolong the conversation. Thlucco was stolidly bent upon doing as he pleased, and the only thing for Sam to do was to take care to conceal the guns from the observation of anybody who might happen to visit the camp.

Thlucco went to town every day and enlisted anew, only to desert with his gun each time. Finally he enlisted twice in one day, and the next day three times, bringing to Sam a gun for each enlistment. By the end of the week Sam had an armory of ten new rifles, with a store of ammunition for each. Thlucco could not count very well, and it required a good deal of persuasion on Sam's part to induce him to stop enlisting. He was persuaded at last, however, that there were more than enough guns in camp to arm the whole party, and then he consented to remain away from the town.

On the evening of the sixth day of their stay in the fishing camp, the boys were just sitting down to their supper of fried fish, when a familiar voice said :—

" I think you might make room for me."

" Bob Sharp back again, as sure's we're here!" exclaimed Billy Bowlegs, and all the boys rose hastily to greet their comrade.

CHAPTER XIX.

SAM SEEKS INFORMATION IN THE DARK.

HY, Bob, old fellow, how are you?"

"You don't mean to say you've got back agin?"

"How'd you find it in the woods?"

These and a dozen other questions were asked while poor Bob's hand was wrung nearly off.

"Now, see here," said Bob, "I can't answer a dozen questions at once. Besides, I've got despatches for the Captain.

"Have you?" asked Sam. "Let me have them, then."

Bob handed Sam an official looking document, which was merely an acknowledgment of his service, a request that he should not abate his diligence, and an instruction to use his own discretion in the conduct of his expedition. Then followed questions and answers innumerable, and the boys learned that General Jackson was in Mobile, without an army, and likely to be without one until the Tennessee volunteers should arrive.

Supper over, Sam quietly informed the boys that he was going into the town, and that he could not say when he should return.

"What're you a goin' to town this time o' night for?" asked Sid Russell, who was strongly prejudiced against staying awake a moment later than was necessary after the sun went down.

"I've laid some plans to get some information," replied Sam, "and I'm going after it," and with that he jumped into the boat, with only Tom for company. In truth, Sam had been in search of the information that he was going after for several days, and he had reason to hope that he might get it on this particular night.

He had already learned that several of the British vessels, now lying in the bay, had sailed away some little time before, and that they had returned on the night before Bob's arrival. He knew that their voyage must have had some connection with the plans they had laid for operations against the American coast, and he thought if he could discover the nature and purpose of this recent expedition, it would give him a clew to their projects for the future. To accomplish this he had taken many risks while the ships were away, and he was now going to try a new way of getting at facts.

He sailed his boat up to the town, and before landing, said to Tom :—

"When I'm ashore, you put off a little way from land and lie-to for an hour or so. When I want you, I'll come down here to the water's edge and whistle like a Whip-Will's Widow. When you hear me, run ashore. If I don't come by midnight, go back to camp, and march at once for Mobile."

"Why can't I lie here by the shore till you come. You're going into danger and may need me."

"First, because there are ruffians around here who might put you ashore and steal the boat ; but secondly, because I don't want to excite suspicion by having our boat seen around here at night. It's so dark that nobody can recognize her if you lie-to a hundred yards from shore. I'm going into danger, but you can't help me."

Avoiding further parley, Sam jumped ashore, and walked quietly up into the town, through the main street, until he came to a house built after the Spanish model, with a rickety stair-way outside. Up this stair-way he climbed, and when he had reached the top he pushed the door open and entered. He found himself in a dark passage, but by feeling he presently discovered a door. As he opened it he said:—

"It's a dark night."

"Is it dark?" answered a voice from within.

"It is very dark."

All this appeared to be merely a pre-arranged signal, for it had no sooner been uttered than the owner of the voice within, who seemed satisfied of Sam's identity, struck a light, with flint and steel, and carefully closed the door.

The man was apparently a dark mulatto, and his hair was matted about his head as if with some glutinous substance.

"You sent me this note?" asked Sam.

"Yes, I gave it to the Injin. He said you'd help me."

There was a brogue in the man's voice, very slight,—too slight, indeed, to be represented in print,—and yet it was perceptible, and it attracted Sam's attention. Perhaps he would scarcely have noticed it but for the fact that all his senses were keenly on the alert. He was not at all sure that he was acting prudently in visiting this man. He had no knowledge whatever of the man, except that Thlucco had somehow found him and arranged a meeting. Thlucco had brought Sam a scrap of dirty paper, on which were traced in a scarcely legible scrawl, these words:—

"Your man must say, 'It's a dark night!' I'll say, 'Is it dark.' We will know each other then."

In delivering this note, with directions as to the method of finding the man, Thlucco had said:—

"Injun no fool. Injun know m'latter man. M'latter man tell Sam heap. Sam take m'latter man way."

By diligent questioning, Sam had made out that this man had knowledge of affairs in the British camp which he was willing to sell for some service that Sam could do him.

Sam was not sure of Thlucco. His knowledge of the Indian character did not predispose him to trust Indian professions of friendship, and he strongly suspected treachery of some sort here. He thought it possible that this was only a scheme to entrap his secret and himself, and he had gone to the conference determined to be on his guard, and in the event of trouble, to use the stout cudgel which he carried as vigorously as possible.

"If we are to talk," he said to the man, "you must come with me."

The man hesitated, afraid, apparently, of treachery.

"I do not know you," he said, "and the Indian may have lied."

"Listen to me," said Sam in reply, "I do not know you, and the Indian may have lied to me. Yet I have trusted myself here in the dark. You must trust something to me. Go with me, and when we have talked together for an hour, if you wish to return here, I pledge you my word of honor, as a gentleman's son, to bring you back safely. If you will not go with me, we may as well part at once. I positively will not say another word. I'm going. Follow me in silence, or stay here, as you please."

With that Sam opened the door and walked out. The man quickly extinguished the light and crept after Sam, in his bare feet.

Sam led the way by a route just outside the town, without exchanging a word with his companion. Half an hour's walking brought them to the lonely strip of beach on which Sam had landed.

"Whip-Will's Widow," whistled Sam, shrilly.

His companion started back in affright, and was on the point of running away, when Sam seized him by the arm, and, shaking him vigorously, said :—

"I'll not play you false. Trust me. I have a boat here."

"You come from the Fort?" said the man in abject terror.

"No, I do not. I am an American," said Sam, no longer hesitating to reveal his nationality, now that he saw how terrified the man was at thought of falling into British hands.

The words re-assured the man, and when Tom

came ashore with the boat he embarked without further hesitation.

"Beat about, Tom," said Sam, "I may have to land again. I have promised this man to return him safely to the place in which I found him, if we don't come to some agreement. Sail around here while we talk."

Turning to the man, he said:—

"Let us talk in a low voice. Who are you, and what?"

"I'm a deserter from the marine corps."

"British?"

"Yes. I'm an Irishman. I've blacked my hair and skin, that's all."

"When did you desert?"

"Yesterday. I was to be flogged for insubordination, and I jist run away."

"Were you with the late expedition?"

"Yes."

"Very well. I think we can come to an understanding. You want to get away, out of reach of capture?"

"Sure I do. If I'm caught, I'll be shot without mercy."

"Very well. Now if you'll tell me everything you know, I'll help you to get away. More than that, I'll get you away, within our own lines. I have the means at my command."

"Faith an' I'll tell you everything I ever know'd in my life, if you'll only get me out of this."

The man was now in precisely the mood in which Sam wished to have him. He had already confessed his desertion, and had now every reason to speak freely and truly, and it was evident that he meant to do so.

"Tom," said Sam.

"Well," replied Tom.

"You may beat up toward our camp, now."

"And you'll save me?" asked the man, seizing Sam's hand and wringing it.

"I will. Now let's come to business."

"I'm ready," answered the man.

"Where did the ships go?"

"To the Island of Barrataria."

"To treat with Jean Lafitte, the pirate?" exclaimed Sam.

"Yes, to enlist him and his cut-throats in the war against you."

"Did they succeed?"

"I don't know. The officers dined with Lafitte, and treated him like a prince. They came away in good spirits, and must have succeeded, else they'd a' been glum enough."

"What do they propose to do next?"

"They're a goin' to sail again in a few days, and the boys say it's for Mobile this time. The men had orders yesterday to get ready."

"What preparation are they making?"

"They're storing the ships and taking water aboard. The marines are kept in quarters on shore, and a lot o' them red savages is in camp at the fort, with Captain Woodbine in command."

"Well, now," said Sam, "tell me why you think the next movement will be against Mobile? May it not be New Orleans instead?"

"Well, you see them pirates is wanted for the New Orleans work. They know all the channels, and have got the pilots. When the fleet starts for New Orleans some o' them 'll be on board. Besides, the officers talk over their rum, and the men hear 'em, an' all the talk is about Mobile, and Mobile Point, whatever that is; so its pretty sure they're going to Mobile first."*

By this time the boat, which was running under a good stiff breeze, ran upon the beach by Sam's camp, and Sam led the way to the dying camp fire, which he replenished, for the sake of the light. Then getting his writing materials he prepared a despatch to General Jackson. It ran as follows :—

CAMP NEAR PENSACOLA,
September 8th, 1814.

TO MAJOR-GENERAL JACKSON,
Commanding Department of the South-West.

GENERAL :—

I beg to report that several of the British vessels of war now lying at anchor in the harbor of Pensacola, have just returned from a brief voyage, the object and nature of which I have endeavored to discover. I have succeeded in finding a deserter from the British marine corps, from whom, under promise of protection, I have drawn such information as he possesses. He accompanied the late expedition, and tells me that it went to the Island of Barrataria, to seek the assist-

---

* It is scarcely necessary to tell readers who are familiar with American History, that Jean Lafitte was not properly a pirate, although he was called so in 1814; nor is it necessary to tell here how the British attempt to use his lawless band against the Americans miscarried. All that belongs to the domain of legitimate history.

ance of Jean Lafitte, the pirate, and his gang of outlaws, against the United States. Whether the negotiations to that end were successful or not, he does not know, but he supposes, from the temper in which the officers returned, that they were.

From this deserter I learn, also, that preparations are making for a hostile movement, which the British marines and soldiers believe, from the remarks made by officers in their presence, is to be directed against Mobile by way of Mobile Point, which I take to be the point of land which guards the entrance to Mobile bay, where Fort Bowyer stands.

I send the deserter with the messenger who takes this to you, partly because I have promised to secure him against recapture, and partly because you may desire to question him further.

There are no present appearances of the immediate sailing of this expedition, but from what the deserter tells me, I presume that it will sail within a few days. I shall remain here still, to get what information I can, and will report to you promptly whatever I learn. I cannot say how long I shall be able to stay, as a British officer visited my camp yesterday, and questioned my boys, as I thought, rather suspiciously. I shall be on the alert, and take no unnecessary risk of capture.

All of which is respectfully submitted.

SAMUEL HARDWICKE,
Commanding Scouting Party.

CHAPTER XX.

A SUSPICIOUS OCCURRENCE.

HEN Sam had finished his despatch he quietly aroused Bob Sharp and Sidney Russell, and entered into conversation with them.

"Sid," he said, "I have a prisoner and a despatch of very great importance to send to General Jackson. You must take the despatch and leave as soon as possible, with the prisoner, whc is a deserter and who must be got away from here before daylight. Bob, I want you to give Sid as good directions as you can, as you've been over the route twice."

"Yes an' I've sort o' blazed it too, and picked out all sorts o' land-marks to steer by, but I don't know's I can make any body else understand 'em. Are you in a big hurry with the despatch?"

"Yes, the biggest kind. It's of the utmost importance, and time is every thing. A single hour lost may lose Mobile or a battle."

"Then maybe Sid an' me'd both better go,—Sid to do the fast running an' me to show him the way."

"There's no use of both of you going," replied Sam, "but if you had had a couple of days rest I would send you instead of Sid, because you know the way, and I don't believe anybody can make the distance any quicker than you have done it."

"I know a feller that kin," replied Bob.

"Who is it?" asked Sam.

"Me."

"You? How do you mean?"

"I mean that I kin go to Mobile most a day quicker 'n I dun it before. I got into a lot o' tangles before that I know how to keep out of now."

"Yes, but you can't start back again without at least a day's rest."

"Can't I though? I'm as fresh as an Irish potato without salt, an' if you just say the word,

I'll be off the minute you git your papers ready. The boys have got somethin' cooked I reckon."

Sam complimented Bob upon his vigor and readiness, and accepted his offer. Ten minutes sufficed for all necessary preparations, and Bob was about starting with his prisoner, when Sid Russell spoke.

"I say, Sam, did you say this 'ere feller's a deserter?"

"Yes. What of it?"

"Nothin', only there's a camp o' British an' Injuns back there a little ways, an' if Bob don't look out he'll run right into it."

"A camp? Where?" asked Sam.

"Right in rear of us, not three hundred yards away."

"When was it established there?"

"To-night, just after you went away in the boat."

"All right," replied Sam. "Jump into the boat, Bob, and we'll sail down below and you can start from there."

It was easy enough to carry Bob and the deserter down to a point below the camp, but

Sam was not at all pleased to find the British so near him. He feared already that he was suspected, and he was not sure that this placing of troops near him was not a preparation for something else. At all events, it was very embarrassing, for the reason that it would prevent him from withdrawing his party suddenly to the woods on their retreat, if anything should happen, and this made Sam uneasy. He returned to camp, after parting with Bob and the deserter, and sat for an hour revolving matters in his mind.

At first he was disposed to wake the boys and quietly withdraw by water to a point lower down, but upon reflection he was convinced that his removal by night immediately after the troops had been stationed near him, would only tend to excite suspicion. He thought, too, that he must have been wrong in supposing that the camp had been established in rear of him with any reference to him or his party.

" If they suspected us in the least, they would arrest us without waiting to make sure of their suspicions," he thought; nevertheless, it was awkward to be shut in and cut off from the easy retreat which he had planned, as a means of escape, in the event of necessity, and he determined to seek an excuse for removing within a day or two from his present camping place to one which would leave him freer in his movements. He was so troubled that he could not sleep, and the flickering blaze of the dying camp fire annoyed him. He got up, therefore, from his seat on a log and went to the boat and sat down in the stern sheets to think.

He had no fear of danger for himself, or rather, he was prepared to encounter, without flinching, any danger into which his duty might lead him; but I have not succeeded very well in making my readers acquainted with Sam Hardwicke's character, if they do not know that he was a thoroughly conscientious boy, and from the beginning of this expedition until now, he had never once forgotten that his authority, as its commander, involved with it a heavy responsibility.

"These boys," he frequently said to himself, "are subject to my command. They must go where I lead them, and have no chance to use their own judgments. I decide where they shall go and what they shall do, and I am responsible for the consequences to them."

Feeling his responsibility thus deeply, he was troubled now lest any mistake of his should lead them into unnecessary danger. He carefully weighed every circumstance which could possibly affect his decision, and his judgment was that his duty required him to remain yet a day or two in the neighborhood of Pensacola, and that it would only tend to awaken suspicion if he should remove his camp to any other point on the shores of the bay. He must stay where he was, and risk the consequences. If ill should befall the boys it would be an unavoidable ill, incurred in the discharge of duty, and he would have no reason, he thought, to reproach himself.

Just as he reached this conclusion, Thlucco came from somewhere out of the darkness, and stepping into the boat took a seat just in front of Sam, facing him.

"Why, Thlucco," exclaimed Sam, "where did you come from?"

"Sh—sh—," said Thlucco. "Injun know. Injun no fool. Injun want Sam."

"What do you want with Sam?"

"Sam git caught! Injun no fool. Injun see.'

"What do you mean, Thlucco? Speak out. If there is any danger, I want to know it."

"Ugh! Injun know Jake Elliott!"

"What about Jake?" asked Sam.

"Um, Jake Elliott *devil.* Jake hate Sam. Jake hate General Jackson. Injun no fool. Injun see."

Sam was interested now, but it was not easy to draw anything like detailed information out of Thlucco.

"What makes you think that, Thlucco? What have you seen or heard?"

"Um. Injun see. Injun know. Injun no fool. Jake cuss Sam. Jake cuss Jackson. Injun hear."

"When did you hear him curse me or General Jackson, Thlucco?" asked Sam.

"Um. To-day! 'Nother day, too! 'Nother day 'fore that."

"What did he say?"

"Um. Jake *cuss.* Um. Jake gone."

"What!" exclaimed Sam. "Gone! where?"

"Um. Injun don't know. Injun know Jake gone."

"When did he leave camp?"

"Um. When Sam go 'way Jake go too! Injun follow Jake. Jake cuss Injun. Injun come back."

"Is that all you know, Thlucco?"

"Um. That's all. That's 'nough. Jake gone 'way."

Sam jumped out of the boat and waked the boys.

"Where did Jake Elliott go to-night?" he asked.

None of the boys knew.

"Did any one of you see him leave camp?"

"Yes," answered Billy Bowlegs, "but we didn't pay much attention to him. He's been so glum lately that we've been glad to have him out of sight."

"Has he ever gone away before?" asked Sam.

"No, only he never stays right in camp. He sleeps over there by them trees," said Billy Bowlegs, pointing to a clump of trees about forty or fifty yards away, "an' I guess he's only gone over there. He never stays with us when you're not here."

Sam strode over to the trees indicated, and searched carefully, but could find no trace of Jake there. Returning to the camp he asked :—

"Did any of you observe which way he went when he went away?"

"Yes," answered Sid Russell, "he went toward his trees."

"That is toward the town," answered Sam.

"Yes, so it is."

"Have you observed anything peculiar about his conduct lately?"

"No," replied Billy Bowlegs, "only that he's been a gettin' glummer an' glummer. I'll tell you what it is, Captain Sam, I'll bet a big button he's deserted an' gone home. He's a coward and he's been scared ever since he found out that you wa'n't foolin' about this bein' a genu-*ine*, dangerous piece of work, an' I'll bet he's cut his lucky, an' gone home, an' if ever I get back there I'll pull his nose for a sneak, you just see if I don't."

"Very well," said Sam, "go to sleep again,

then. If he has gone home it is a good riddance of very bad rubbish."

Sam was not by any means satisfied that Jake had gone home, however. Indeed he was pretty well convinced that he had done nothing of the sort, and he wished for a chance to think, so that he might determine what was best to be done. He believed Jake would not dare to go home as a deserter, knowing very well what reputation he would have to bear ever afterward, in a community in which personal courage was held to be the first of the virtues, and the lack of it the worst possible vice. Where had he gone, then, and for what? Sam did not know, but he had an opinion on the subject which grew stronger and stronger the more he revolved the matter in his mind.

Jake Elliott, he knew, had a personal grudge against him, and no very kindly feeling for the other boys. He was confessedly afraid to continue in the service in which he was engaged, and it was not easy for him to quit it. There was just one safe way out of it; and that offered, not safety only, but revenge of precisely the kind that Jake Elliott was likely to take. Sam knew very well that, notwithstanding his magnanimity, Jake still bitterly hated him, and still cherished the design of wreaking his vengeance upon him at the first opportunity.

"What is more probable, then," he asked himself, "than that Jake is trying to betray us into the hands of the enemy to die as spies? He is abundantly capable of the treachery and the meanness, and his desertion of the camp to-night strongly confirms the suspicion."

This much being decided, it was necessary for Sam to determine what should be done in the circumstances. If there had been no camp in his rear, he would have withdrawn his command through the woods at once. As it was, he must find some other way. It was clearly his duty to escape with his boys, if he could, and to lose no time in attempting it. The danger was now too near at hand, and too positive to be ignored, and there was really very little more for him to do here. He must escape at once.

But could he escape?

That was a question which the event would have to answer, as Sam could not do it. He could

Unluckily, it was already beginning to grow light, and he would not have the shelter of darkness.

He aroused the boys again, before they had had time to get to sleep, and quietly began his preparations.

"Make no noise," he said, "but put what provisions you have, and all your things into the boat. *Don't forget the guns and the ammunition.* Sid! take our little water keg and run and fill it with fresh water."

The boys set about their preparations hurriedly, although they but dimly guessed the meaning of Sam's singular orders.

At that moment Jake Elliott shuffled into the camp.

CHAPTER XXI.

JAKE ELLIOTT MAKES ANOTHER EFFORT TO GET EVEN.

S it is impossible to tell at one time the story of the doings of two different sets of persons in two different places, it follows that, if both are to be told, one must be told first and the other afterward.

For precisely this reason, I must leave Sam and his party for a time now, while I tell where Jake Elliott had been, and what he had been about.

When Sam let him off as easily as he could at the time of the compass affair, and even went out of his way to prevent the boys from referring to that transaction, he did so with the distinct purpose of giving Jake an opportunity and a motive to redeem his reputation; and he sincerely hoped that Jake would avail himself of the chance.

It is not easy for a man or boy of right impulses to imagine the feelings, or to comprehend the acts of a person whose impulses are all wrong, and so it was that Sam fell into the error of supposing that his badly behaved follower would repent of his misconduct and do better in future. This was what all the boys thought that Jake ought to do, and what Sam thought he would do; but in truth he was disposed to do nothing of the sort, and Sam was not very long in discovering the fact. Instead of feeling grateful to Sam for shielding him against the taunts of his companions, he hated Sam more cordially than ever, when he found how completely he had failed in his attempt to embarrass the expedition. He nursed his malice and brooded over it, determined to seize the first opportunity of "getting even," as he expressed it, and from that hour his thoughts were all of revenge, complete, successful, merciless. He was willing enough, too, to include the other boys in this wreaking of vengeance, as he included them now in his malice.

His first attempt to accomplish his purpose, as we know already, was an effort to wreck the boat in a drift pile, and that affair served to open Sam's eyes to the true character of the boy with whom he had to deal. He trusted him no more, and managed him thereafter only by appeals to his fears.

When the camp was formed near Pensacola, Sam carefully canvassed the possibilities of Jake's misconduct, and concluded that the worst he could do would be to injure the boat or her tackle, and he sufficiently guarded against that by always sleeping near the little craft.

Jake was more desperately bent upon revenge than Sam supposed, and from the hour of going into camp he diligently worked over his plan for accomplishing his purpose. He had learned by previous failures, to dread Sam's quickness of perception, of which, indeed, he stood almost superstitiously in awe. He would not venture to take a single step toward the accomplishment of the end he had set himself, until his plans should be mature. For many days, therefore, he only meditated revenge not daring, as yet, to attempt it by any active measures. At last, however, he was satisfied that his plans were beyond Sam's power to penetrate, and he was ready to put them into execution. On the night of Bob Sharp's return, which was the night last described in previous chapters, Sam went to the town, as we know, accompanied by Tom, who sailed the boat. As soon as he was fairly out of sight Jake walked away toward Pensacola. The distance was considerable, and the way a very difficult one, as the tide was too high for walking on the beach, so that it was nearly midnight when Jake knocked at a house on a side street.

"Who is there?" asked a night-capped personage from an upper window.

"A friend," answered Jake.

"What do you want?" said the night-capped head, rather gruffly.

"I want to see the Leftenant."

"What do you want with me?"

"I want to talk with you."

"Oh, go to the mischief! I'm in bed."

"But I must see you to-night," said Jake.

"On business?"

"Yes, sir."

"Important?"

"Yes."

"Won't it keep till morning?"

"No, sir; I'm afraid not."

"Very well. I suppose I must see you then. Push the door open and find your way up the stairs."

Jake did as he was told to do, and presently found himself in the room where Lieutenant Coxetter had been sleeping. That distinguished servant of His Majesty, King George, had meantime drawn on his trowsers, and he now lighted a little oil lamp, which threw a wretched apology for light a few feet into the surrounding darkness.

"Now then," said the officer, in no very pleasant tones, "What do you want with me at this time o' night? Who are you, and where do you come from?"

Jake was so nervous that he found it impossible to find a place at which to begin his story, and the impatient Lieutenant spurred him with direct questions.

"What's your name?" he asked. "You can tell that, can't you?"

"Yes, sir," faltered Jake

"SPEAK, MAN! OR I CHOKE YOU."

"Well, tell it then, and be quick about it."

"My name is Jacob Elliott," said that worthy, fairly gasping for breath in his embarrassment.

"Oh! you do know your name, then," said the officer. "Now, then, where do you come from?"

"From Alabama," answered Jake.

"From Alabama! the mischief you do! You're an American then? What the mischief are you doing here?"

"Oh, sir, that's just what I want to tell you about, if you'll let me."

"If I'll *let* you? Ain't I doing my very best to *make* you? Havn't I been worming your facts out of you with a corkscrew? But you'd better be quick about giving an account of yourself If you don't give a pretty satisfactory one, too, I'll arrest you as a *spy*,— a *spy*, my good fellow, do you understand? *A spy*, and we hang that sort o' people. Come, be quick."

"Spies! that's just it, Lieutenant. I came here to-night to tell you about spies."

"Then why the mischief don't you do it? You'll drive me mad with your halting tongue. Speak man, or I'll choke you!" and with that the officer stood up and bent forward over Jake, to that young man's serious discomfiture.

"They's some spies here—," Jake began. "Where?" asked the impatient officer interrupting him.

"Down there, in a camp," said Jake, talking as rapidly as he could, lest the officer should interrupt him again; "Down there in a camp by the bay, an' they've got a boat an' guns, an' they're boys, an' they pretend to be a fishin' party."

"Ah!" said the Lieutenant, "I thought I'd make you find your tongue. Now listen to me, and answer my questions, and mind you don't lie to me, sir; mind you don't lie."

"I won't. I pledge you my honor—," began Jake.

"Never mind pledging that; it isn't worth pledging. You see you're a sneak, else you wouldn't be here telling tales on your fellow countrymen. But never mind. It's my business to make use of you. I'm provost-marshal."

This was not at all the sort of treatment Jake had expected to receive at the hands of British officers. He had supposed that the value of his services in betraying his fellows, would be recognized and rewarded, and he had even dreamed of receiving marked attentions and a good, comfortable, safe place in the British service in recompense. It had never occurred to him that while all military men must get what information they can from deserters, and traitors, they do not respect the sneaking fellows in the least, but on the contrary hold them in profoundest contempt, almost spurning them with their boots. Jake had gone too far to retreat, however, and must now tell his whole story. He told where the boys were, and how they had come there, and for what purpose, lying only enough to make it appear that he himself had never willingly joined them, but had been deceived at first, and forced afterward into the service.

The Lieutenant listened to the story and then asked :—

"Have you anything to show for all this?"

"How do you mean?" asked Jake.

"Why, you wretched coward, don't you understand? How am I to know how much of your story is true, and how much of it false? Of course it isn't all true. You couldn't talk so long without telling some lies. What I want to know is, what can you show for all this story? If I arrest these boys, what can be proved on them?"

"Well, the Captain's got a despatch from General Jackson; that'll prove something."

"When did he get it?"

"To-night."

"Very well. That's something. Now you just sit still till I tell you to do something else."

So saying the Lieutenant summoned a courier or two, and sent them off with notes.

"These boys have a boat, you say?"

"Yes."

"Do they know how to sail it?"

"A little; the Captain handles it better'n the rest."

"Has he ever been to sea?"

"No, sir."

"What sort of a boat is it?"

"A dug-out; we made it ourselves."

"Oh, did you? Why didn't you tell me that first? Never mind, it's all right. They'll never try to put to sea in a dug-out, but they may try to escape to some point lower down the bay in it, so my message to the fort won't be amiss."

The Lieutenant had sent a message to the fort that at daylight he should arrest the party, and that if they should take the alarm and try to escape by water, a boat must be sent from the fort to overhaul them.

He now dressed himself, first sending for a file of soldiers under a sergeant, with instructions to parade at his door immediately.

When all was ready he said to Jake.

"Now then, young man, come with me, and guide me to the camp of these lads."

Jake led the way, and when a little after daylight they approached the camp the Lieutenant said to him :—

"I don't want to make any mistake in this business. You go ahead to the camp and see if the lads are there. That'll throw 'em off their guard, and I'll come up in five minutes."

"But Lieu—" began Jake, remonstratingly.

"Hold your tongue, and do as I tell you, or I'll string you up to a tree, you rascal."

Thus admonished, Jake walked on in fear and

trembling to the camp. As he approached it he observed the unusual stir which was going on, and wondered what it meant, but he did not for a moment imagine that Sam had guessed the truth.

CHAPTER XXII.

THE SEA FIGHT.

WHEN Jake entered the camp it was fairly light, and as Sam looked at him he caught a glimpse of the file of soldiers in the thicket, three or four hundred yards away.

He knew what it meant.

"We're about to leave this place, Jake," said Sam, as the boys stowed the last of their things in the boat, "we're about to leave this place, and you're just in time. Get in."

"Well, but where—" began the culprit.

"Get in," interrupted Sam, who stood with one of the rifles in his hands.

Jake hesitated, and was indeed upon the point of running away, when Sam, placing the muzzle of his gun almost against Jake's breast, said:—

"Get into the boat instantly, or I'll let daylight through you, sir."

There was no help for it, and Jake obeyed.

Sam quickly cast the boat loose, and as he did so, the Lieutenant discovered his purpose, and started his men at a full run toward the camp.

Sam pushed the boat off and, taking his place in the stern, took the helm.

" Hoist the sail, quick !" he said; and the sail went up in a moment. A strong breeze was blowing and the sail quickly bellied in the wind.

" Lie down, every man of you," cried Sam, but without setting the example. A moment later a shower of bullets whistled around his ears. He had seen that the soldiers were about to fire upon him, and had ordered his companions to lie down, confident that the thick solid sides of the boat would pretty effectually protect them.

As for himself, he must take the chances and navigate his boat. The soldiers were not more than fifty yards from him when they fired but luckily they failed to hit him.

"Now for a run!" he exclaimed. "Before they can load again, I'll be out of range, or pretty nearly."

The breeze was very fresh, almost high, and

as the boat got out from under the lee of the shore timber, she heeled over upon one side, and sped rapidly through the water. The Lieutenant made his men fire again, but the distance was now so great that their bullets flew wide of the mark.

"We're off boys at last. Look out for Jake Elliott and don't let him jump overboard, or he'll swim ashore. He is a prisoner."

"Is he? what for?" asked Billy Bowlegs.

"For betraying us to the British."

At this moment a boat pushed out from the dock at the fort, and Sid Russell, who was Sam's most efficient lieutenant, and was scanning the whole bay for indications of pursuit, cried:

"There goes a row boat out from the fort, Sam, an' they's soldiers on board 'n her. I see their guns."

"Arm yourselves, boys," was Sam's reply. "I want to say a word first. Jake Elliott has betrayed us to these people, and they are trying to arrest us. If they catch us, we shall be treated as spies; that is to say, we shall be hanged to the most convenient tree. I believe we're all the sons of brave men, and ready to die, if we must, but I, for one, don't mean to die like a dog, and for that reason I'll never be taken alive."

"Nor me," "nor me," "nor me," answered the boys, neglectful of grammar, but very much in earnest.

"Very well, then," replied Sam. "It is under stood that we're not going to surrender, whatever happens."

"It's agreed," answered every boy there except the wretched prisoner, who was no longer counted one of them.

"That boat has no sail," said Sam, "and she's got half a mile to row through rough water before she crosses our track half a mile ahead. I think I can give her the slip. If I can't we'll fight it out, right here in the boat. Now, then, one cheer for the American flag!" and as he said it, Sam drew forth a little flag which he had carried in all his wanderings, for use if he should need it, and ran it up to his mast head by a rude halyard which he had arranged in anticipation of some such adventure as this.

The boys gave the cheer from the bottom of

their broad chests, and every one took the place which Sam assigned him, with gun in hand. Meantime Sam tacked the boat in such a way as to throw the point of meeting between her and the British boat as far from the fort as possible. It was very doubtful whether he could pass that point before the row boat, propelled by six oars in the hands of skilled oarsmen, should reach it. If not, there remained only the alternative of "fighting it out."

"Reserve your fire, boys, till I tell you to shoot. There are only six armed men in that boat. If they shoot, lie down behind the gunwale. You mustn't shoot till we come to close quarters. Then take good aim, and make your fire tell. A single wasted bullet may cost us our lives. Above all, keep perfectly cool. We've work to do that needs coolness as well as determination."

The boats drew rapidly nearer and nearer the point of meeting, and Sam saw that he would succeed in passing it first, but narrowly, he thought.

"We'll beat them, boys," he said. "The sea

is rough, and they can't do much at long range, and they won't get more than one shot close to us." At that moment the men in the British boat fired a volley, after the manner which was in vogue with British troops at that day. The two boats were not a hundred yards apart, but the roughness of the water, on which the row boat bobbed about like a cork, rendered the volley ineffective.

"They're good soldiers with an idiot commanding them," said Sam.

"Why?" asked Tom, who was very coolly studying the situation.

"Because he made them fire too soon," replied Sam, "and we can slip by now while they're loading. Don't shoot, Joe!" he exclaimed to the black boy who was manifestly on the point of doing so. "Don't shoot, we've got the best of them now; we are past them and making the distance greater every second. Give them a cheer to take home with them. Hurrah!"

It was raining now, and the wind was blowing a gale, so that Sam's boat was running at a speed which made pursuit utterly hopeless. The British soldiers fired three or four scattering shots, and then cheered in their turn, in recognition of the admirable skill and courage with which their young adversary had eluded them.

Sam's escape was not made yet, however. A war ship lay below, and her commander seeing the chase, and the firing in the bay, manned a light boat with marines, and sent her out to intercept Sam's craft, without very clearly understanding the situation or its meaning.

Sam saw this boat put off from the ship, and knew in an instant what it meant. He saw, too, that he had no chance to slip by it as he had done by the other, as it was already very near to him, and almost in his track.

"Now, boys," he said very calmly, "we've got to fight. There's no chance to slip by that boat, and we've got to whip her in a fair fight, or get whipped. Keep your wits about you, and listen for orders. Cover your gun pans to keep your priming dry. Here, Tom, take the tiller. I must go to the bow."

Tom took the helm, and as he did so Sam said to him.

"Keep straight ahead till I give you orders to change your course, and then do it instantly, no matter what happens. I've an idea that I know how to manage this affair now. You have only to listen for orders, and obey them promptly."

"I'll do what you order, no matter what it is," said Tom, and Sam went at once to the bow of his boat.

His boys were crouching down on their knees to keep themselves as steady as they could, and their guns, which they were protecting from the rain, were not visible to the men in the other boat, who were astonished to find that they had, as they supposed, only to arrest a boat's crew of unarmed boys.

The boats were now within a stone's throw of each other, the English boat lying a little to the left of Sam's track, but the officer in command of it, supposing that the party would surrender at the word of command, ordered his men not to open fire.

"They's a mighty heap on 'em for sich a little boat," whispered Sid Russell.

"So much the better," said Sam. "They're badly crowded."

Then, turning to his companions, he said:—

"Lie down, quick, they'll fire in a moment."

The boys could see no indication of any such purpose on the part of the British marines, but Sam knew what he was about and he knew that his next order to his boys would draw a volley upon them.

Turning to Tom, and straightening himself up to his full height, while the British officer was loudly calling to him to lie to and surrender, Sam cried out:

"Jam your helm down to larboard, Tom, quick and hard, and ram her into 'em!"

Tom was on the point of hesitating, but remembering Sam's previous injunction and his own promise, he did as he was ordered, suddenly changing the boat's course and running her directly toward the British row boat, which was now not a dozen yards away. The speed at which she was going was fearful. The British, seeing the manœuvre, fired, but wildly, and the next moment Sam's great solid hulk of a boat struck the British craft amidships, crushed in her sides, cut her in two, and literally ran over her.

"Now, bring her back to the wind," cried Sam, "and hold your course."

The boat swung around and was flying before the wind again in a second. Boats were rapidly lowered from the war ship to rescue the struggling marines from the water into which Sam had so unceremoniously thrown them.

" Three cheers for our naval victory, and three more for our commodore!" called out Billy Bowlegs, and the response came quickly.

" It's too soon to cheer," said Sam. " We're not out of the scrape yet."

The next moment a puff of smoke showed itself on the side of the war ship and a shower of grape shot whizzed angrily around the boat. A second and a third discharge followed, and then came solid shot, sixty-four pounders, howling like demons over the boys' heads, and plowing the water all around them. Their speed quickly took them out of range, however, and the firing ceased.

They now had time to look about them and estimate damages. None of the solid shot had taken effect, but three of the grape shot had struck the boat, greatly marring her beauty, but doing her no serious damage.

"Are any of you hurt?" asked Sam. All the boys reported themselves well.

" Then make a place for me in the middle of the boat, where I can lie down," replied Sam, " I'm wounded."

" Where ? "

" How ? "

" Not badly, I hope, Sam ? " the boys answered quickly.

" I'm hurt in two places. They shot me as we ran over that boat," said Sam, " but not very badly, I think. I'm faint, however," and as he lay down in the boat he lost consciousness.

CHAPTER XXIII.

CAPTAIN SAM.

THE boys were now badly frightened, and the more so because they did not know what to do for their chief, who lay dying, as they supposed. His left hand and shoulder were bleeding profusely, and Tom, remembering some instructions that Sam had once given him* with respect to the stopping of a flow of blood, at once examined the wounds, to discover their nature. Two fingers of Sam's left hand had been carried away, and a deep flesh wound showed itself in his shoulder. By the use of a handkerchief or two Tom soon succeeded in staunching the flow of blood, while one of the other boys sailed the boat. After a little while the dashing rain revived the wounded boy, and while he was still very weak,

---

* See "The Big Brother" Chapter 3.

he was able, within an hour, to take the direction of affairs into his own hands again.

But what mischief may be done in an hour! The boys had never once thought of anything but Sam, during all that time, and they had been sailing for an hour straight out into the Gulf of Mexico, at a furious rate of speed! It was pouring down rain, and land was nowhere visible!

When Sam's questions drew out these facts, the boys were disposed to be very much frightened.

"There's no cause for alarm, I think," said Sam, reassuringly. "I think I know how to manage it, and perhaps it is better so."

"Of course you know how to manage," said Sid Russell, admiringly. "I'm prepared to bet my hat an' boots on that, now or any other time. You always do know how to manage, whatever turns up. That long head o' your'n's got more'n a little in it."

Sam smiled rather feebly and replied:—

"Wait till I get you out of the scrape we're in, Sid, before you praise me."

"Well, I'll take it on trust," said Sid, "an' back my judgment on it, too."

"Let me have your compass, Tom," he said; and taking the instrument which he had confided to Tom's hands at starting on the voyage, he opened his map just enough to catch a glimpse of the coast lines marked on it, having one of the boys hold a hat over it, to protect it from the rain as he did so. After a little while he said:—

"Take the helm, Tom, and hold the boat due west. There, that will do. Now let her go, and keep her at that. The wind is north-east, and she'll make good time in this direction."

"Where are you aiming for, Sam?" asked Tom.

"The mouth of Mobile Bay."

"Does it lie west?"

"Not exactly, but a little north of west. We can sail faster due west, however, and after a while we'll tack to the north till we see land. It's about forty miles from the mouth of Pensacola Bay to the mouth of Mobile bay, and we're going, I think, about six or seven miles an hour."

"But, how'll you find the mouth of the bay?"

"I don't know that I can, but I can find land

easily enough, as it stretches in a bow all along to the north of us. But I want to strike as near the mouth of the bay as I can, so as to have as little marching to do as possible. If I can get into the bay, I can sail clear up to Mobile."

"But, Sam?"

"Well."

"What if it storms? It looks like it was going to."

"Well, I think we can weather it. This boat can't spring a leak, and if she fills full of water she won't sink, for she's only a log hollowed out."

"That's so, but won't she turn over like a log?"

"I think not. She's heaviest at the bottom, and I made her keel very heavy on purpose."

"Why, did you expect to go to sea in her?"

"No, but I thought I might have to do it, to get away from Pensacola."

"Did you think of that when you planned her, up there in the woods?"

"Yes."

"Yes," said Sid, "of course he did! Don't he always think of every thing before it comes?"

It was rapidly coming on to storm. The rain was falling very slightly now, and the wind was shifting to the east and rapidly rising. Sam directed the boys to shorten sail, and showed them how to do it. The wind grew stronger and stronger, suddenly shifting to the south. The sail was still further shortened. The sea now began coming up, and Sam saw that their chief danger was that of getting washed overboard. He cautioned the boys against this, and changed the boat's course, so as to keep her as nearly as possible where she was. A heavy sea broke over her, and carried away their only water keg, which was a dire calamity. After a little while their store of food went, and they were at sea, in a storm, without food or water!

"I say, Sam," said Tom.

"What is it?"

"Is there land all to the north of us?"

"Yes."

"How far is it?"

"Twenty miles, perhaps,—possibly less."

"Why can't we head the boat about, and run for it?"

"Because the wind is blowing on shore, and there's a heavy surf running."

"What of that?"

"Why, simply this, that if we run ashore on a long, flat beach, the boat will be beaten to splinters a mile or more from land."

"How?"

"By the waves; they would lift her up, and receding let her drop suddenly on the sands, splitting her to pieces in no time, and the very next wave would do the same thing for us. We must stay out here till the storm's over. There's nothing else for it."

The storm lasted long enough to make a furious sea, and the boys could do nothing but hold on to the boat's gunwales. As night came on the wind ceased, very suddenly, as it frequently does in Southern seas, but the waves still rolled mountain high.

"When the sea goes down we'll try to make land, won't we, Sam?" asked Tom.

"Yes, but before the surf is safe for us, we can

sail several hours toward Mobile, and gain that much. Indeed, I think we can get that far west before it will be tolerably safe to run ashore. We're hungry and thirsty, of course, but we must endure it. There's no other way."

The boat was presently headed to the west, and the sail unfurled again, but as the night advanced the wind fell to a mere breeze, and then died altogether. It began to grow hazy. The haze deepened into a dense fog. The sea went down, and the boat rocked idly on a ground swell.

"Now, let's run ashore," said Billy Bowlegs.

"What will we run with? There isn't a cap full of wind on the Gulf of Mexico, and there won't be while this fog lasts."

"What shall we do, then?"

"Nothing, for there is literally nothing to be done," answered Sam.

"Mas' Sam," said Joe, "I'll tell you what."

"Well, Joe, what is it?"

"Ef we jist had a couple o' paddles."

"But we just haven't a couple of paddles," answered Sam. "No, what we need now is courage and endurance. We must wait for a wind, and keep our courage up. We are suffering already with hunger and thirst, and will suffer more, but it can't be helped. We must keep our courage up, and endure that which we cannot do anything to cure. It is harder to endure suffering than to encounter danger, but a brave man, or a brave boy, can do both without murmuring."

Sam's words encouraged his companions, and they managed to get some sleep. After awhile day dawned, and the fog was still thick around them, while not a zephyr was astir. Nearly an hour later, a sudden booming startled them. It was a cannon, and was very near.

"What is that?" asked the boys in a breath.

"A sunrise gun, I think," said Sam, "and it's on a ship or a fort. Now then all together with a shout."

They shouted in concert. No answer came. They shouted again and again, and finally their shout was answered. A little later a row boat came out into the fog, and the first man Sam saw in it was Tandy Walker.

It is not necessary to repeat the greetings and

the explanations that were given. Sam learned that the gun had been fired from Fort Bowyer, the guardian fortress, which, standing on Mobile Point, commanded the entrance to the bay. The fort had been garrisoned only the day before, and Tandy was one of the garrison. Sam's boat had drifted further west than he had supposed, and he found himself now precisely at the point he had tried to reach.

As Sam was too weak to walk, and there was no wind with which to sail up to the town, a messenger was sent by land from the fort, bearing to General Jackson a detailed account of Sam's wanderings and adventures in the shape of a written report. When the wind served, the little band of weary wanderers sailed up to Mobile, and when Sam reached the hospital to which he had been assigned for the treatment of his wounds, he found there an official despatch from General Jackson, from which the following is an extract:—

"The commanding General begs to express his high sense of the services rendered by Samuel Hardwicke and his band, and his appreciation of the rare courage, discretion and fortitude displayed by the youthful leader of the Pensacola scouting party. A few blank commissions in the volunteer forces having been placed in the commanding General's hands for bestowal upon deserving men, he is greatly pleased to issue the first of them to Mr. Hardwicke, in recognition of his gallant conduct, creating him a captain of volunteers, to date from the day of his departure on his recent mission."

"So, you're really 'Captain Sam' after all," said Sid Russell, when the document was read in his presence, and the formal commission had been inspected reverently by all the boys.

"Yes, an' he's been a real 'Captain Sam' all the time," said Billy Bowlegs.

What became of Jake Elliott?

If he had been an enlisted soldier he would have been tried by court martial. As it was, the boys formally drummed him out of their company, and he disappeared from Mobile. He did not go home as the boys learned a few months later, when, after the battle of New Orleans, peace was proclaimed throughout the land, and they were led back by their favorite hero, Captain Sam.

THE END.

Putnams' Series of Popular Manuals.

HALF-HOURS WITH THE MICROSCOPE. By EDWIN LANKESTER, M.D., F.R.S. Illustrated by 250 Drawings from Nature. 12mo, cloth, $1.25.

"This beautiful little volume is a very complete manual for the amateur microscopist. * * * The 'Half-Hours' are filled with clear and agreeable descriptions, whilst eight plates, executed with the most beautiful minuteness and sharpness, exhibit no less than 250 objects with the utmost attainable distinctness."—*Critic.*

HALF-HOURS WITH THE TELESCOPE: Being a popular Guide to the Use of the Telescope as a means of Amusement and Instruction. Adapted to inexpensive instruments. By R. A. PROCTOR, B.A., F.R.A.S. 12mo, cloth, with illustrations on stone and wood. Price, $1.25.

"It is crammed with starry plates on wood and stone, and among the celestial phenomena described or figured, by far the larger number may be profitably examined with small telescopes."—*Illustrated Times.*

HALF-HOURS WITH THE STARS: A Plain and Easy Guide to the Knowledge of the Constellations, showing in 12 Maps, the Position of the Principal Star-Groups Night after Night throughout the Year, with introduction and a separate explanation of each Map. True for every Year. By RICHARD A. PROCTOR, B.A., F.R.A.S. Demy 4to. Price, $2.25.

"Nothing so well calculated to give a rapid and thorough knowledge of the position of the stars in the firmament has ever been designed or published hitherto. Mr. Proctor's 'Half-Hours with the Stars' will become a text-book in all schools, and an invaluable aid to all teachers of the young."—*Weekly Times.*

MANUAL OF POPULAR PHYSIOLOGY: Being an Attempt to Explain the Science of Life in Jntechnical Language. By HENRY LAWSON, M.D. 18mo, with 90 Illustrations. Price, $1 25.

Man's Mechanism, Life, Force, Food, Digestion, Respiration, Heat, the Skin, the Kidneys, Nervous System, Organs of Sense, &c., &c., &c.

"Dr Lawson has succeeded in rendering his manual amusing as well as instructive. All the great facts in human physiology are presented to the reader successively; and either for private reading or for classes, this manual will be found well adapted for initiating the uninformed into the mysteries of the structure and function of their own bodies."—*Athenæum.*

WOMAN BEFORE THE LAW. By JOHN PROFFATT, LL.B., of the New York Bar.

CONTENTS.—I. Former Status of Women. II. Legal Conditions of Marriage. III. Personal Rights and Disabilities of the Wife. IV. Rights of Property, Real and Personal. V. Dower. VI. Reciprocal Rights and Duties of Mother and Children. VII. Divorce.

12mo, cloth, $1. Half bound, $1.25.

BASTIAT. SOPHISMS OF PROTECTION. By FREDERIC BASTIAT. With Preface by HORACE WHITE. Cloth. Price $1.00.

REEVES. The Students' Own Speaker. A Manual of Oratory By Paul Reeves. 12mo, boards, 75 cts.; cloth, 90 cts.

The "Student's Own Book," by Paul Reeves, which forms the first of the Handy-Book Series, is notable among other points in giving "a good deal for the money." The amount of matter in this book, which is in clear and neat, though small type, fully equals that in other books of twice the size and cost. It contains many new pieces not to be found in any of the school text-books. It aims to meet the wants of a large number outside of the school-room, while it is also well adapted for school use.

The *Philadelphia Inquirer* says of it:

"The general rules laid down, and the suggestions thrown out, are excellent, while the pieces furnished for declamation are well chosen. The book is one deserving a wide circulation."

Another good authority says:

"We have never before seen a collection so admirably adapted for its purpose. Prose and verse, humor, eloquence, description, alteration, burlesque discourse of every kind. . . . For schools, clubs, and fireside amusement, it will be found an almost inexhaustible source of entertainment. . . . The instruction . . . is sensible and practical."

RICHARDSON. House Building. From a Cottage to a Mansion. A Practical Guide to Members of Building Societies, and all interested in selecting or Building a House. By C. J. Richardson, Architect, author of "Old English Mansions." With 600 illustrations. Crown 8vo, cloth extra, $3.50.

RITCHIE. The Romance of History—France. By Leitch Ritchie. Illustrated. 12mo, cloth extra, $2.50.

ROGERS. Social Economy. By Prof. E. Thorold Rogers (Tooke Professor of Economic Science, Oxford, England), editor of "Smith's Wealth of Nations." Revised and edited for American readers. 12mo, cloth, 75 cts.

This little volume gives in the compass of 150 pages, concise yet comprehensive answers to the most important questions of Social Economy. The relations of men to each other, the nature of property, the meaning of capital, the position of the laborer, the definition of money, the work of government, the character of business, are all set forth with clearness and scientific thoroughness. The book, from its simplicity and the excellence of its instruction, is especially adapted for use in schools, while the information it contains is of value and interest to all classes of readers.

"It is this sort of knowledge that is contained in Prof. Rogers' book, which we cannot too highly recommend to the use of teachers, students, and the general public."—*American Athenæum.*

ROGERS. The Poetical Works of Samuel Rogers. Including "Italy," "Columbus," "Pleasures of Memory," etc., with portrait. 12mo, cloth extra, $1.50; half calf, $3.50.

SEGUIN. A Manual of Thermometry. For Mothers, Nurses, and all who have charge of the Sick and the Young. By Edward Seguin, M.D. 12mo, cloth, 75 cts.

www.ingramcontent.com/pod-product-compliance
Lightning Source LLC
LaVergne TN
LVHW011206110826
845150LV00006B/1336
* 9 7 8 1 4 2 5 5 1 9 0 3 2 *